HOME TO WICKHAM FALLS

BY
ROCHELLE ALERS

MILLS &
BOON

First Published in Great Britain 2017
By Mills & Boon, an imprint of HarperCollins*Publishers*
1 London Bridge Street, London, SE1 9GF

© 2017 Rochelle Alers

ISBN: 978-0-263-92315-5

23-0717

Since 1988, national bestselling author **Rochelle Alers** has written more than eighty books and short stories. She has earned numerous honors, including the Zora Neale Hurston Literary Award, the Vivian Stephens Award for Excellence in Romance Writing and a Career Achievement Award from *RT Book Reviews*. She is a member of Zeta Phi Beta Sorority, Inc., Iota Theta Zeta Chapter. A full-time writer, she lives in a charming hamlet on Long Island. Rochelle can be contacted through her website, www.rochellealers.org.

Home to Wickham Falls is dedicated to my editor,
Megan Broderick.
Thank you for your patience and the wonderful
chats that helped to breathe life into this story.

Better a dry crust with peace and quiet than a house full of feasting, with strife.

Chapter One

"With a show of hands, how many want to delay going public until after the summer?" Two of the three software engineers sitting at the table raised their hands along with Sawyer Middleton. "The ayes have it." He saw the withering look Elena Ng-Fitzgerald gave her husband. Thom was the only one who hadn't raised his hand, and they needed a majority vote to go from a privately held company to a public one.

If the decision of the majority of the partners had gone the other way, Sawyer had been mentally prepared to deal with the outcome of selling shares of their internet company.

He took a sip from an oversized mug filled with coffee. The meeting that began at six that morning was approaching the four-hour mark. He would have suggested breaking for a least an hour, but knew the other three did not want to lose their momentum. The meeting's agenda focused on whether to take the software company public, and if not, then whether or not to go on hiatus while offering their employees the summer off with pay before starting up again after Labor Day.

The sixteen employees connected to the software company thought of themselves as an extended family, spending more time with one another than their own families. And it was normal for Sawyer to put in a seventy-hour workweek now that he was no longer dating.

His cell phone vibrated and he glanced at the number on the screen. A slight frown creased his forehead when he saw his sister's number. Sawyer stood. "Sorry, guys, but I have to take this," he said, picking up the phone. "What's up, Rachel?" he asked quietly, as he walked out of the room.

"Dad had a heart attack last night. I'm at the hospital with him now."

Sawyer sucked in a breath. "How is he?"

"The surgery was successful. He had two blocked arteries. Right now he's in the ICU."

Although he and Henry Middleton were like oil and water, Sawyer knew he had to be there, if not for his father, then for his mother and sister. "How's Mom holding up?"

"She's a mess, but she's trying to keep it together for the boys. Colin and Dylan left yesterday afternoon for an overnight camping trip with their Boy Scout troop. They're supposed to be back tonight around eight."

"I'll be there as soon as I can book a flight."

"Text me when you get to the hospital. And thanks, Sawyer."

"There's no need to thank me, Rachel. Even though

Dad and I don't see eye-to-eye on a lot of things, he's still my father. I don't want you or Mom to tell him I'm coming." He ended the call and then returned to the conference room. "I have to go home. My father had a heart attack, and I'm not sure when I'll be back."

Thom stood up. "Don't worry about it, Saw. We've already delayed going public, and anyway we're all going to take a break at the end of the month. I'm just sorry yours has to begin with a family emergency."

One by one the others approached Sawyer, giving him a comforting pat on the back. Elena went on tiptoe and brushed a kiss on his stubble. "Go home and pack. I'll call the travel agency and have Shirley schedule your flight and ground transportation. She'll ring your cell as soon as everything is confirmed."

Sawyer kissed her forehead. "Thanks, beautiful." Elena blushed as she ducked her head.

"Let us know one way or the other about your father," Darius said.

Sawyer forced a smile. "I will."

Ninety minutes later Sawyer mounted the steps to the private jet at a New Jersey regional airport. He was one of a half-dozen passengers. The first stop was Charleston, West Virginia, where Sawyer would pick up a rental for the drive to Wickham Falls.

A flight attendant showed him to his seat. "As soon as we're airborne lunch will be served. You'll find the menu in the seat pocket."

Sawyer flashed a polite smile. "Thanks, but I'm going to pass on lunch."

He didn't need food as much as he needed to sleep. It had been more than three years since he'd returned to

Wickham Falls, and the day he walked out of the house where he'd grown up, his father forbade him to darken his door again. Sawyer experienced some guilt about staying away so long, despite his father's mandate, because he missed seeing his mother, sister and nephews.

Sawyer closed his eyes as the jet taxied down the runway, and he didn't open them again until they were airborne. Then he reclined his seat and fell asleep. It felt as if they had just lifted off when the pilot's voice came throughout the cabin informing the flight crew to prepare for descent. The aircraft landed smoothly on a runway at the Charleston airport where a driver waited to take Sawyer to an area where he could pick up a rental car.

It was mid-May and his favorite time of the year in West Virginia. Everything was lush, and afternoon temperatures were warm enough for short sleeves. He stored his luggage in the back of the Jeep and drove south toward Wickham Falls. The familiar sight of mountains transported him back to his childhood, when he spent time fishing and swimming in a nearby lake and exploring Native American foot trails.

Sawyer had cherished every day, whether rain or shine, that his merchant-seaman father was out to sea. His mother hummed as she went about her housework, the house was filled with the mouth-watering aromas of baking cookies, and his younger sister and her girlfriends giggled uncontrollably at any- and everything. But that all changed the instant Henry came home.

An hour later he turned into visitor parking at the Johnson County Medical Center and sent Rachel a text that he was in the parking lot; seconds later she returned it indicating she was in the nurse's lounge and would meet him at the front desk.

The instant Sawyer walked into the lobby and saw his sister he felt worse for not coming home sooner. She was thinner than the last time he saw her, and even at that time she could ill afford to lose weight. Her slight frame appeared lost in a pair of pink scrubs. And as he came closer he saw the dark shadows under her blue-gray eyes. Either she was working too hard or not getting enough sleep. He extended his arms and wasn't disappointed when she moved into his embrace. Resting a hand on her back, Sawyer pressed a kiss to her mussed dark red hair.

"Hey, baby sister."

Rachel Phelan smiled. "I didn't expect you to get here until sometime tonight."

"I was lucky to get a flight leaving this afternoon."

Rachel gave Sawyer a lingering stare.

"Even though it's not visiting hours I can get you up to see him. He probably won't be able to talk because he's been sedated."

"I'll see him when he's alert."

Rachel frowned. "Why can't you forgive him for sending you away?"

"It's not about forgiveness. He is who he is and I am who I am. I'll stay until he's medically cleared, then I'm going back to New York."

"That may not be for several weeks."

Resting a hand in the small of his sister's back, he steered her toward the exit. "Then I'll stay until he's cleared."

"Can you afford to stay away from your company for an extended period of time?"

Reaching for Rachel's hand, Sawyer gave her fingers a gentle squeeze as he led her to the rental. "Have you forgotten I'm my own boss?"

Rachel nodded as she pulled her hand from his loose grip. "My car is in the employees' lot. I volunteered to work a double tonight because the weekend neonatal nurse has a family emergency."

"Leave it. I'll drive you back in time for your shift. Besides, you look exhausted. When was the last time you had at least eight hours of sleep?" Sawyer asked.

Rachel closed her eyes for a few seconds. "I can't remember. I come home to see the boys off to school, and then go to bed, but I don't sleep well because sometime I can hear Dad and Mom fussing over nonsense."

Opening the passenger-side door, Sawyer assisted Rachel up, and then slipped out of his jacket. "Do you want to leave?"

The seconds ticked as sister and brother stared at each other. "I don't want to move to New York."

"I'm not talking about New York. What if I help you buy a house here?"

Waiting until Sawyer rounded the Jeep and slipped behind the wheel, Rachel said, "No. I'm not going to borrow any more money from you." She had moved out of the house she'd rented after her divorce and back in with her parents in order to make ends meet.

Punching the Start engine button, Sawyer shifted into gear. "Stop it, Rachel," he admonished softly. "I'm fortunate enough to make a lot of money, and if I can't help my sister and nephews then what good am I? I told you before, any money I give you, you don't have to pay back."

"I don't want you to think of me as a charity case, Sawyer."

Sawyer clamped his jaw tightly. He did not tell Rachel that he had set up custodial bank accounts in her sons' names because he did not want her ex to slack off on his less-than-adequate child support payments. And he doubted whether he would ever have to pinch pennies. The four-story loft building had been his only big-ticket purchase. It was across the street from Enigma4For4; he occupied the two top floors and leased the two lower floors to an art gallery and an architectural design firm.

Out of the corner of his eye, Sawyer saw Rachel staring at him. "What's the matter?"

"Are you dating anyone?"

He shook his head.

"What happened to that girl you saw for more than a couple of months?"

A derisive sneer twisted his mouth. "We broke up six months ago."

"What happened?"

Sawyer's fingers tightened on the steering wheel. "She wanted a baby and I told her I'm not ready to become a father."

"When do you think you're going to be ready? At forty? Or maybe fifty?"

"Very funny, Rachel."

"I'm not trying to be funny. You're thirty-three, and it seems as if you're becoming more and more anti-marriage. Do you even like women, other than to sleep with them?"

"I can assure you, little sister, that I like women a lot. Just not the ones who try to force me to do something I'm not ready to do."

"So, you're telling me if you met a woman you really like you'd marry her, like, yesterday?" She snapped her fingers.

"I'd have to do more than like her because I'd never marry a woman I didn't love."

"Are you saying there *is* the possibility that one of these days you'll make me an auntie?" Rachel asked, smiling.

He returned her smile. "Maybe."

"What aren't you telling me, big brother?"

Sawyer sobered and concentrated on the road. He wanted to tell Rachel there was nothing to tell. He wasn't dating anyone and he wondered whether he'd become too comfortable with his own company or just more discriminating.

"It's going to be a while before I consider becoming a father."

"How long is a while? And why wouldn't you want to have children?"

A noticeable muscle twitched in Sawyer's jaw when he clenched his teeth. "I didn't say I don't want children, it's just that I don't want to raise my kids like Dad."

Rachel exhaled an audible breath. "Didn't you say Dad is who he is and you are who you are? And that means you could never be like him." She paused. "You should know he hasn't been the same since you left The Falls."

"And that means what?"

"That he's mellowed. And when he barks at Mom she comes right back at him."

Sawyer flashed a wide grin. "Wonders never cease. I figured after a while she'd get tired of being his doormat."

"There are times when she's like a junkyard dog barking at him and refusing to back down. She told me once she turned fifty-five she wasn't taking it anymore."

Although he avoided verbal confrontation, Sawyer would give anything to witness his mother standing up to her husband. "It looks as if you have company," he said, as a late-model gray Ford Escape maneuvered into the driveway behind his father's decades-old red pickup.

"That's Jessica. She was the boys' second grade teacher. She's probably here to drop off the books I asked her to bring for their summer reading. Now that they're going into middle school I don't want them to lag behind."

Sawyer pulled in alongside the SUV and shut off the engine. "I thought they were good students."

"They're above grade level in every subject but language arts. I preach until I'm blue in the face that they have to stop playing those darn computer games and read more."

"That's easy enough to fix. Use your parental controls," Sawyer suggested. "I'll…" His words trailed off when his nephews' former teacher got out of her car and came around to the passenger-side door.

He was unable to pull his gaze away from the slender legs in sheer navy-blue stockings and matching silk-covered stilettos. His gaze moved up to a body-hugging sleeveless black dress ending at her knees, banded at the neckline and around a slightly flaring hem in the same shade as her footwear. Rachel was out of the rental and exchanging hugs with the young woman.

The brilliant afternoon sun glinted off Jessica's black pixie-cut hairstyle, and when she turned to look at him Sawyer felt as if he had been punched in the gut. During his time in the military he'd seen countless beautiful women from every race and ethnic group, yet there was something about the woman smiling at him that made him feel like a gauche adolescent when he could not pull his gaze away from the perfection of the round brown face with large dark eyes, an enchanting button-like nose and generously curved lips outlined in a glossy red-orange lipstick. Her features were reminiscent of a delicate doll's, and there was something about her face that reminded him of a darker version of Salma Hayek. His movements were robotic as he stepped out of the vehicle, unaware he had been holding his breath until he felt the constriction in his chest.

Looping an arm through Jessica's, Rachel met Sawyer's eyes. "Sawyer, I'd like you to meet Jessica Calhoun."

Jessica's smile grew wider as she extended her hand. "It's nice to finally meet you. Rachel talks about you all the time."

Sawyer took the proffered hand. Everything about her was sensual, including her perfume, along with her sultry voice. "I hope the talk has been more good than bad."

There was beat, then Jessica said, "She adores you."

His gaze swung to Rachel who appeared embarrassed as evidenced by the blush suffusing her cheeks. "And I adore her."

"May I have my hand back please?" Jessica whispered, smiling.

Sawyer had forgotten he was still holding on to her hand. "Sorry about that,"

"I'm sorry to hear about your father."

He inclined his head because he didn't have a comeback. If his father had not had a heart attack Sawyer doubted he would have ever returned to Wickham Falls as long as Henry Middleton was alive.

Jessica turned, opened her SUV's passenger-side door, scooped up the canvas bag resting on the seat and handed it to Rachel. "These are the books for Dylan and Colin. Sawyer, if you don't mind, could you please get the picnic hamper from the cargo area?"

"No problem." He walked to the rear of the vehicle and, grasping the handles on the covered wicker hamper, lifted it easily. "Where do you want this?"

"You can take it into the house."

"What did you bring?" Rachel asked Jessica.

"I decided to make a few dishes for your mother. With your dad in the hospital I figured she's not going to have a lot of time cooking for the family."

Rachel glared at Jessica. "You didn't have to do that," she chided sotto voce.

A slight frown settled between Jessica's eyes. "Please, Rachel. Don't start. I told your mother about it. If I can't help out friends in a family crisis then I'm not much of a friend. I only came by to drop off the books and the food. I have to head out now or I'll be late for the retirement dinner. Nice meeting you, Sawyer," she called out as he headed for the house.

Sawyer stopped, turned and flashed a warm smile at the same time he hoisted the hamper to a shoulder. "Nice meeting you, too." He was still standing in the same spot when Jessica drove away.

"Be careful, brother. You were staring at Jessica like a deer caught in the headlights," Rachel teased.

"That's because she's stunning," he replied, walking toward the house, Rachel following.

"I thought you were partial to tall, skinny blondes.

Correct me if I'm wrong, but I've never known you to date women from other races."

"You *are* wrong. Since living in New York I've dated women across racial and ethnic lines."

Rachel gave him a sidelong glance. "You've really changed."

Sawyer opened his mouth to tell his sister that he really had not changed that much when the front door opened and his mother stepped out onto the porch. He knew his absence had impacted his mother more than Rachel or even his nephews because Mara Middleton told him that she sometimes cried after their telephone conversations ended. Those were the times when he had to force himself not to leave New York to return to his hometown. But now he was back to reconcile his past and make peace with his father. Even if it meant groveling, he would put aside his pride to make it a reality.

Taking long strides, he mounted the steps to the porch, set the hamper on a table and swept his mother up in his arms. Except for a few more silver strands in her dark hair, Mara Middleton hadn't changed much.

"How long are you staying?" Mara asked.

Sawyer kissed her forehead. "How long do you want me to stay?"

Mara eased back, her smoky-gray eyes filling with tears. "You're not playing with me, are you?" she asked.

He kissed her again, this time on both cheeks. "No, Mom. I'm not playing with you. I'll stay as long as you need me."

Her arms tightened around his neck. "What I'd really like is for you to move back to Wickham Falls."

He would spend as much time needed to reunite and hopefully heal his fractured family, and when it came time for him to return to New York it would not be with the heavy heart he'd felt more than three years before. "Moving back is not an option, but I'm willing to stay for the summer."

Mara pushed against her son's shoulder. "I suppose the summer is better than nothing. Now, please put me down so I can get a good look at you. FaceTiming isn't the same as seeing you in person." She rested a hand along his jaw. "You look good, son." She stroked the curling strands on his nape.

"So do you," Sawyer countered. He hadn't lied to his mother. The stress and turmoil of attempting to maintain a peaceful household had not taken a toll on her pretty face. He stared over her head, frowning. He rocked back and forth when the porch's floorboards moved under his weight. He also noticed a few shutters had come loose from their fastenings and all were in need of a new coat of paint. "Why does this place look so run-down?"

Mara's eyelids fluttered. "We'll talk about that later. Let's go inside and put away the food Jessica brought over. She volunteered to cook for us because she knew Rachel and I said we were going to take turns hanging out at the hospital until Henry's discharged."

His strained expression was replaced by astonishment. "She would do that?"

"Have you been away so long that you've forgotten that folks in The Falls look out for one another?"

Sawyer forced a smile. "I suppose you can say I have."

Coming home this time would be different than when had been honorably discharged from the army. Then he had planned to stay and put down roots in his hometown. However, the constant warring between himself and his father had made that impossible.

Mara opened the screen door, holding it ajar as he picked up the hamper and walked back into the house he'd sworn he would never reenter.

Chapter Two

Sawyer set the hamper on a bench in the corner of the immaculate kitchen. It had been updated during his absence. New kitchen appliances had replaced old and brand-new flooring had been exchanged for worn tiles. "I'm going back to the car to get my bags."

"I hope you don't mind, the boys are now in your old bedroom," Mara said. "I had Henry take your bed up to the attic once Rachel moved back. We also put in a bathroom with a vanity, commode and shower because I thought the boys would want to sleep up there. But they much prefer your room because it's large enough for twin beds."

Sawyer gave his mother a tender smile. "It doesn't matter where I sleep, Mom."

Mara returned his smile. "Are you hungry?"

"Yes."

"Go bring your bags in. You can eat while I make up your bed."

"I do know how to make up a bed, Mom."

"I know you do, Sawyer," she countered. "I just need to keep busy."

"What you need to do is relax. Once Dad is given a clean bill of health the two of you need to go away for an extended vacation."

"That's not going to happen until we make repairs to the outside of the house."

Now Sawyer knew why the exterior was in disrepair. His father didn't like loans, and he waited until he saved enough money to pay for an earmarked project. Sawyer left the kitchen through a side door. Although Henry had sailed to ports all over the world, his wife had yet to travel out of the country. She occasionally went to see her twin sister in Ohio but that wasn't what Sawyer deemed a vacation. If Henry had mellowed, as Rachel claimed, then Sawyer would try and convince him to take his wife away for a little R & R for their upcoming thirty-fifth wedding anniversary.

Sawyer removed his bags from the Jeep's cargo area and returned to the house. Within seconds of walking into the kitchen he inhaled aromas that reminded him of how long it had been since he'd eaten. "Something smells delicious."

"I just reheated Jessica's baked chicken in the microwave," Mara said as she ladled a spoonful of potato salad onto the plate with the chicken and a slice of cornbread. "I don't know what she uses to season it, but I could eat her chicken every day."

Sawyer washed his hands in the small bathroom off the kitchen, a ritual he'd followed since childhood. Rachel entered the kitchen as he sat at the table. She'd changed out of her scrubs and into a pair of shorts and baggy T-shirt.

"Do you want me to fix you a plate, too?" Mara asked her daughter.

"No, thanks," Rachel replied, peering at the labeled containers on the table. "I grabbed a bite at the hospital. I just came down to tell you I'm going to bed and locking my door so the boys don't barge in."

"Don't worry, sis, I'll make certain they won't bother you."

Wrapping her arms around Sawyer's neck, Rachel dropped a kiss on his hair. "I still can't believe you're here."

He patted her hand. "Believe it."

Sawyer could not believe it, either. His mind was flooded with wonderful memories of himself and Rachel sitting at the kitchen table enjoying an afternoon snack before doing homework while Mara busied herself making dinner. It was the good memories rather than the disturbing ones that kept him from totally despising his father.

He cut into a piece of chicken and popped it into his mouth. "Oh, my goodness! This chicken is incredible!"

Mara gave him a knowing smile. "Now you know what I'm talking about."

Hard-pressed not to moan out his pleasure while savoring the most delicious baked chicken he had ever had, Sawyer concentrated on finishing the food on his plate. It appeared Jessica was the total package. She had looks, brains *and* she could cook! Although he considered himself a modern man with passable culinary skills, he still preferred women with the ability to put together a palatable meal.

There was something about Jessica that intrigued Sawyer, and he didn't need his sister's assistance as a go-between to get to know her. The odds were in his favor that their paths would cross again.

Jessica had been driving for ten minutes when her attention shifted from the road to the navigation screen as Rachel's number appeared. She tapped the Bluetooth feature on the steering wheel. "Yes!" she answered cheerfully.

"I can't believe you made so much food." Rachel's voice came clearly through the speaker. "When did you find the time to make potato salad and potpies?"

"It's not that much food. I had leftover chicken, so instead of making a salad I decided to make potpies because they're Colin and Dylan's favorites."

Every day of the school year she devoted to a particular task. Saturdays were set aside for cleaning the house and cooking enough meals for the entire week. Although she lived alone and at thirty-one hadn't had a serious relationship in years, there was never a time when she experienced bouts of loneliness. And now that she'd rescued a black-and-white bichon frisé–poodle mix from a shelter, the house was filled with barking.

Rachel's voice broke into her musings when she said, "You spoil my boys so much that one of these days I'm going to drop them on your doorstep with a note that you can keep them for the summer vacation."

Jessica chuckled softly. "That'll work. I'll teach them how to grow their own food. And I'm certain they'll enjoy playing with Bootsy."

There was a noticeable pause from Rachel before she said, "I know you get tired of hearing it, and you've told me more than once that I'm a busybody, but it's time you think about getting married so you can have a couple of babies and stop spoiling other folks' kids."

"You know that's not going to happen until I meet a man I can trust enough to fall in love with him. Besides, I have a baby who wakes me up every morning while demanding all my attention the moment I walk through the door."

"I'm not going to fight with you when I say a dog cannot replace—"

"Then don't!" Jessica retorted angrily. A swollen silence filled the car. "I'm sorry, Rachel. I shouldn't have snapped at you. You know why I don't trust men, so if I really want to become a mother then I'll adopt." She drove over a railroad crossing.

"There has to come a time when you have to forgive and forget about the folks who blamed you for testifying against the man who raped your college roommate."

"You sound like my former therapist."

Rachel's laugh came through the speakers. "That's because we're each other's therapist."

She and Rachel had become each other's sounding boards and confidantes after Rachel volunteered as a class mother. Once Dylan and Colin were promoted to the third grade, Jessica bonded with their mother. "You're right, Rachel. But sometimes it's hard to forget that the man that I loved beyond belief and was engaged to marry blamed me for ruining his best friend and fraternity brother's life."

"If he chose his frat brother over you, then you're better off without him."

"I know that now."

"I've learned to forgive Mason for not being here for me and our children, because whenever I look at my boys I see him in them. But it wasn't until after I divorced him that I realized I could make it on my own."

Signaling, Jessica maneuvered onto the road leading to the interstate. This year, with a dozen teachers retiring, the district had decided to hold the farewell festivities at a hotel a mile off the West Virginia Turnpike. "You have made it, Rachel."

"Not completely."

"Why would you say that?"

"I don't want you to breathe a word of this to anyone, not even my mother, but Sawyer sends me money every month to supplement what Mason sends for child support. I was able to catch up on my bills, pay credit cards and put money into my savings account for the proverbial rainy day. When I tried to talk to him about sending me so much, he says discussing money is gauche."

"I agree." Jessica had gone to a prestigious all-girl boarding school, and she'd grown tired of some of her classmates' bragging about how much money their families had.

"If that's the case, then you and my brother will get along quite well. Speaking of Sawyer, you'll probably get to see quite a bit of him because he told my mother he plans to be here until Labor Day. Once Colin and Dylan discover their uncle will be here for the summer they're going to be as happy as pigs in slop."

A hint of a smile softened Jessica's mouth. Her former students weren't the only ones looking forward to summer vacation, because she'd begun counting the days to the end of the school year. "Good for them. I'm really looking forward for summer break. This year my students have worked my last nerve."

"No! Not Miss Calm-and-Collected Calhoun."

Jessica made a sucking sound with her tongue and teeth. "I've never before taught a group of students where none of them get along for more than a few hours. It's like witnessing a reenactment of the Hatfields and McCoys."

"Damn-m-m," Rachel drawled.

"No. It's double damn, because detention or sending them to the principal's office doesn't seem to work."

"I had no idea your students were giving you that much trouble."

"I suppose I can't have it easy every year."

Jessica was also looking forward to the summer because she would spend it in Wickham Falls instead of visiting her parents in Seattle, Washington. Her retired college-professor parents had decided to drive up the coast and tour Alaska for the months of June and July.

"I'm going to hang up now and try to get some sleep."

"Call me and let me know when your father can have visitors."

"That probably won't be until he's out of ICU."

"That's okay. Talk to you later."

"Later," Rachel replied.

Jessica disconnected the Bluetooth and then tapped a button for the satellite radio. Instead of her favorite station featuring R & B oldies, she selected one with Rock classics. Bon Jovi's "Living on a Prayer" blared throughout the vehicle. The heavy baseline beat put her in a party mood. Twenty minutes later she left her car with valet parking and walked into the hotel. She almost didn't recognize the middle school's physical education teacher in a dress and heels, because sweats and running shoes doubled as her ubiquitous school uniform.

Three teachers with whom she'd formed a close bond walked into the lobby together. They greeted her with hugs and air kisses while complimenting her on her dress and shoes. It was on very rare occasions Jessica was seen in a dress and heels, which did not lend themselves to teaching second graders.

Once a month Jessica got together with Abigail Purvis, Beatrice Moore and Carly Adams—pre-K, kindergarten and first-grade teachers—for a girls' night out. They alternated eating at her home or in one of the local restaurants before driving to the next town to bowl.

"Let's go in before they run out of the good stuff," said Beatrice, who was the most outspoken of the quartet.

Jessica led the way into the ballroom crowded with school board members, administrators, faculty and staff. She took a flute of champagne off the tray of a passing waiter. The noise was deafening from laughter and those calling out to one another as glasses were raised in celebratory toasts. She had many more years of teaching ahead of her before she put in for retirement. Her eyes met the high school's science teacher as he wended his way toward her.

"When do you think we'll be able to get together to write another grant for the tech lab?" Logan Fowler asked Jessica.

She and Logan chaired the committee that applied for grants to benefit the school district. "Are you available this summer?"

A slight frown furrowed Logan's smooth forehead. "I thought you were going to the West Coast."

During the last committee meeting she had announced she was going to spend the summer in Seattle. "That was before my parents decided they were going to drive up to Alaska."

"I'd like to get a head start on it as soon as possible because I probably won't have much time outside of classes once the new term begins," Logan replied. "I'm also going to be out of the country the month of July. If it's all right with you, I wouldn't mind starting on it next weekend."

When it had come time for Jessica to cochair the committee, she had proposed the district solicit funding for a new technology lab for the elementary and middle schools. "Next weekend is okay with me. We can meet at my place." He leaned closer and kissed her cheek.

Jessica smiled. "By Monday morning it will be all over The Falls that Miss Calhoun is hooking up with Mr. Fowler."

"Let them talk," he whispered.

It was apparent Logan hadn't wanted to disclose the details of his personal life. She had known him to be a very private person until one day he inadvertently mentioned he was going to Paris to visit his girlfriend during spring break.

"Is there something I should know about you and Mister Beautiful?" a familiar voice whispered behind her once Logan was out of earshot. Turning around Jessica glared at the district's nurse.

"I don't know what you're talking about, Hattie." That said, Jessica walked away to eat something to counter the effects of the champagne. She had no intention of discussing her personal life with the woman who probably would put her own spin on anything she said. The Johnson County School District was akin to a small town where gossip spread like a lighted fuse attached to dynamite.

Jessica ignored curious stares as she nibbled on several appetizers. The cocktail hour ended and the waitstaff ushered everyone into the larger ballroom. The retirees were seated on the dais, wearing corsages and boutonnieres in the school's colors. Collectively the twelve had logged nearly four hundred years of educating young people. Jessica could imagine herself sitting on the dais in twenty-four years. She planned to teach for thirty years, retire at age fifty-five and travel around the world. Once she returned to the States she would begin her longtime dream of writing a series of children's books.

Chapter Three

Sawyer did not get to see his nephews until Sunday morning. The bus traveling from the campground had blown a tire and the Scouts had to wait more than three hours for a replacement vehicle. The Scout leader called parents to inform them their sons would be dropped off sometime around midnight. Meanwhile, he had driven Rachel to the hospital for her eleven o'clock shift and by the time he got back to the house Mara had put her exhausted grandsons to bed.

He was lounging in the kitchen enjoying his second cup of coffee when the boys walked in together. They had grown at least a foot in the three years since he last saw them in person, and although they were fraternal twins, the resemblance between them was remarkable the older they became. It was Dylan who noticed him first, his eyes widening in shock as Sawyer stood up.

"Uncle Sawyer?"

"What's up, champ?"

Colin, galvanized into action, raced across the kitchen and launched himself at his uncle. "You came back!"

Sawyer picked up the gangly boy. Dylan was slower reacting as he walked over to join his brother, and Sawyer scooped him up with his free arm, cradling them as he had done when they were younger.

"You're both too heavy to pick up together." Sawyer set Colin on his feet, then Dylan. "How was your overnight camping trip?"

"It was awesome, Uncle Sawyer," Colin answered. "We made a campfire, roasted marshmallows and slept in a tent."

"Some of the boys were scared when they thought they heard wolves, but not me and Colin," Dylan added, his voice rising in excitement.

Sawyer smiled. "It was probably coyotes." He stared at the two boys who were almost an exact image of their father: dark blond hair, hazel eyes and cleft chin. It was impossible for Rachel to forget her ex-husband whenever she looked at their children.

Colin glanced around the kitchen. "Where's Grandma and Grandpa?"

"Grandma took Grandpa to the hospital so the doctor could check his heart."

"Is there something wrong with his heart?" Dylan asked.

"He was having pains in his chest. He'll probably be there for a few days before they say he's okay to come home."

The two boys exchanged a look. "Is that why you

came home, Uncle Sawyer?" Colin asked. "Because Grandpa's heart is sick?"

Sawyer paused. Either he could fabricate a lie or tell the truth, and he decided on the latter. "Yes, Colin. I came home because Grandpa's heart is sick, and I also want to be here for you, Dylan, your mother and grandmother."

"How long are you going to stay?" Dylan questioned.

"How long do you want me to stay?" he countered.

"Forever!" the twins chorused.

A smile found its way across Sawyer's features as he stared at expressions of expectation on his nephews' faces. "Nothing is forever, but I promise that I'll stay until August when you have to go back to school." He glanced at the clock on the microwave. "It's too late for church, so do you want to go to Ruthie's for brunch?"

"Yes!" the twins chorused.

"Put your shoes on and brush your hair."

Ruthie's was a Wickham Falls family favorite. The restaurant offered an all-you-can-eat buffet from eight to eight, seven days a week.

Sawyer placed his mug in the dishwasher and then retreated to his bedroom to slip into a pair of running shoes. He had slept soundly in the converted attic. Scooping up his keys, money clip, credit card case and cell phone off the nightstand, he headed downstairs and met Colin and Dylan as they raced down the staircase in front of him.

"I'm riding shotgun!" Colin shouted.

"Neither of you are riding shotgun," Sawyer warned. "You'll ride in the back *and* wear seat belts. Don't give me that look, Dylan. You guys know when you ride with me you never sit up front."

The two boys, realizing they weren't going to get one over on their uncle, climbed into the rear seats and buckled their seat belts. Sawyer slipped behind the wheel. Staring at the rearview screen on the dash, he backed out of the driveway. He concentrated on the road and knew he couldn't avoid the inevitable. After brunch he planned to see his father.

Jessica waited on line to get a table at Ruthie's. She usually attended her church's early service, but she had gotten up later than usual.

It was now one o'clock and the popular family-style restaurant was nearly filled to capacity.

"Miss Calhoun."

Jessica glanced over her shoulder when she heard the childish voice. There weren't too many places she could go in Wickham Falls where a student or their parents did not recognize her. She noticed Sawyer standing behind his nephews. There was something in the way he stared at her that made her slightly uncomfortable—but not in a bad way. His gaze lingered on her face before slowly moving lower and coming back to meet her eyes.

She smiled at her former students.

"Hello, Dylan." She glanced over at his brother. "How are you, Colin?"

Colin lowered his eyes. "Good."

Her gaze met and fused with Sawyer's penetrating indigo-blue eyes. "Good afternoon, Sawyer." There was a charming roughness about him she found appealing. A lean jaw and strong chin that accentuated a pair of high cheekbones made for an arresting face. She also noticed red streaks in his shoulder-length dark brown hair.

Why, she wondered, did she sound so breathless?

Maybe it had something to do with the number of times Rachel had talked about her brother. Jessica had to admit he was good-looking, but his looks definitely weren't enough to make her heart beat a little too quickly. Although she liked men, she had a problem trusting them.

Sawyer inclined his head, a hint of a smile tugging at one corner of his firm mouth. "Good afternoon, Jessica. Are you waiting for anyone?"

"No. Why?"

"If we sit together we'll get seated faster than if you wait for a table for yourself."

Jessica knew he was right. There were very few tables with seating for two. "Okay."

She watched Sawyer walk to the front of the line to get the hostess's attention, and then return and beckon for his nephews to move ahead of the others standing in line. Jessica went completely still when she felt Sawyer's hand at the small of her back. Everything about him—his heat, the lingering scent of his aftershave and his touch seeped into her, bringing with it a quickening of her breathing. "Tricia has a table for us," he said in her ear.

Holding on to Colin's hand, Jessica steered him toward the hostess's podium, ignoring the angry stares from those still waiting in line. Sawyer paid the prix fixe for two adults and two children. Seconds later a waiter directed them to a table in the middle of the restaurant.

She leaned close to Sawyer. "I'll take Colin and help him select what he wants."

"I'll wait until you get back, then I'll take Dylan."

Sawyer sat at the table with Dylan, his gaze fixed

on Jessica holding a plate as Colin pointed at what he wanted to eat. A pair of cropped stretch khaki slacks, foam-green blouse and black leather mules had replaced the sexy outfit she wore the night before. He found Jessica's face mesmerizing, with or without makeup, and he forced himself not to stare at the curve of her hips in the body-hugging pants.

Dylan patted his uncle's arm. "I'm hungry, Uncle Sawyer."

He ruffled the boy's hair. "As soon as Colin and Miss Calhoun come back it will be our turn to go up."

"They're taking too long."

"Try and be patient, Dylan."

"I can't be patient when I'm hungry because my stomach is talking too loud."

"You can tell your stomach to stop talking because they're coming back now."

Dylan popped up from his chair and raced over to the buffet counter. Sawyer winked at Jessica when she returned to the table with her plate and Colin's. Sawyer helped Dylan make his selections, while he decided on chicken-fried steak with white gravy, mashed potatoes, fluffy biscuits and sweet tea. He was back in the South and the food on his tray made him feel as if he had really come home.

"I'll go and get the drinks," Jessica said as he set his plate on the table.

"We'll go together. You need to let me know when you're going to be home so I can return your picnic hamper," he said as he filled two glasses with milk.

Jessica gave Sawyer a sidelong glance. "I don't have to be home for you to bring it back. You can either leave it at the front door or on the patio."

"And let coons or some other critter get into it?"

"You heard about that?"

"Yep. My mother said she has a problem with raccoons trying to get into the garbage bins. She claims she saw a few during the daylight hours, which means they're probably rabid. Have you been bothered with them?"

"I haven't seen any." Jessica added a splash of cream in her coffee. "I keep Bootsy inside, and whenever I take him out I make certain to carry pepper spray."

"You walk a cat?"

"Bootsy is a dog, not a cat."

"Who ever heard of a dog named Bootsy? What happened to Bruno or even Bruiser?"

"He's too small to be a Bruno or Bruiser."

He wanted to tell Jessica he was only teasing. "I'm sorry," he called out as she turned, heading back to their table.

"No, you're not," she said, not bothering to give him a backward glance.

He quickened his step. "Yes, I am. I apologize for insulting Bootsy."

Dylan took the glass of milk from Sawyer. "Uncle Sawyer, you have to meet Bootsy. He's a cool dog. Right, Colin?"

"Yep," his twin agreed. "Can you please buy us a dog, Uncle Sawyer? We asked Momma but she said she doesn't have the money."

Jessica leaned closer to Sawyer, her shoulder touching his. "See what you've started?" she whispered.

He turned his head, his mouth only inches from Jessica's. At that moment he wanted to kiss her. Not a long, lingering kiss but a mere brushing of lips. Time appeared to have stood still as he found himself caught in a maelstrom of hypnotic longing. He did not want to believe he was thinking of kissing his sister's friend in a public place *and* in front of his nephews.

"We'll talk about that later."

"When later?" Dylan asked.

Sawyer stared at the boy. "I have to talk to your mother first. If she says yes, then we'll contact a breeder and go look for a puppy." He knew Rachel had the money to buy a dog, and suspected she didn't want the responsibility of taking care of the animal once the excitement of having a pet faded for her sons.

"My dog is a rescue from a puppy mill." Jessica peered at Sawyer over the rim of her coffee cup. "There are too many dogs in shelters waiting for good homes. And if they're not adopted, then they'll be put down. I'm seriously thinking of getting another rescue as a companion for Bootsy."

Picking up his knife and fork, Sawyer cut into his steak. When he was his nephews' age he had begged his mother for a dog and most times Mara had had to take care of his pet when he stayed for after-school sports.

"Can I go back for seconds?"

Colin's question broke into Sawyer's musing. "Take your brother with you. And this time try to put something green on your plate." The two boys bolted from the table and dodged diners carrying plates overflowing with food. "How often do you come here?" he asked Jessica.

She touched her napkin to the corners of her mouth. "No more than once or twice a month. I really prefer cooking for myself."

"That's because you are an incredible cook. Who taught you?"

"My grandmother was an art teacher turned caterer and I used to watch her whenever she prepared for a party. What's incredible is that she never had any professional training. Folks would ask for her recipes, but she refused, saying they were family secrets."

"I guess that means you're not going to tell me what seasonings you use on your chicken."

Jessica closed her eyes while affecting a sexy smile. "You guess right."

Sawyer wanted to scream at Jessica not to do that. It was as if she was inviting him to kiss her. He continued to stare at her mouth. "You're tight with Rachel, so that should act as brownie points when it comes to you thinking of us as family."

Jessica rested her left hand on Sawyer's right. "Nice try."

He decided to try another approach. He didn't want to know her family secrets as much as he wanted to know about the woman who seemingly had charmed his family. "How long have you lived here?"

"I moved to The Falls two years ago. Before that I lived in Beckley."

"Beckley is less than a half hour's drive from here."

"I know," Jessica agreed, "but I got tired of renting. There were a few houses on the market but most of them were out of my price range. Then I discovered a foreclosed property over on Porterfield Lane. I negotiated with the bank to buy it, but only if they approved a home improvement loan, and as they say, the rest is history."

"Good for you." Jessica did not know she had just gone up several more points with Sawyer. It was obvious she was quite the businesswoman. Not only was she beautiful, but she was also feminine *and* intelligent. The winning combination was something he'd found missing in some of the women he had dated. He had come back to Wickham Falls to reunite with his family, but making friends with his sister's friend was definitely a plus. Dylan and Colin returned with dishes of lime gelatin and frozen yogurt covered with chocolate syrup and colorful sprinkles. "You said get something green," Colin stated proudly when Sawyer stared at the shaky dessert.

"That I did," he said under his breath, while ignoring Jessica's smug grin. It definitely was a *gotcha* moment.

She pushed back her chair and he stood up at the same time. "I have to leave now. Thank you for brunch."

"Miss Calhoun, can we come see Bootsy?"

Jessica pointed to her mouth and Colin picked up a napkin to wipe the chocolate syrup staining his. "If your uncle Sawyer wants to take you with him when he brings back the picnic hamper, then you and your brother can come and play with Bootsy."

Dylan popped a cube of gelatin into his mouth. "Please, Uncle Sawyer."

Sawyer shook his head. "Do I have a choice?"

"No!" Jessica and the twins said in unison.

"What day is good for you?" Sawyer asked.

"Next Saturday."

Reaching for his cell phone, Sawyer programmed the event into his calendar. "What time?"

"Come any time after noon. And because it's a holiday weekend, I plan to cook outdoors, weather permitting. If you don't have anything planned, then you're welcome to join me and a few of my friends."

He flashed a Cheshire cat grin. "If that's the case, then I'll see you soon."

She waved to her former students. "Don't forget to read for at least thirty minutes a day." The brothers lowered their heads, pretending interest in their dessert.

Crossing his arms over his chest, Sawyer stared at Jessica until she disappeared from his line of sight before retaking his seat. His sister, mother and nephews liked her, and after spending less than an hour with Jessica he also liked her—a lot. "Are you guys finished eating?"

Colin patted his belly over his T-shirt. "I could eat some more but I don't want a tummy ache."

"That means you've had enough. Let's go, champs."

"Where are we going?" Dylan asked.

"Home where you guys can hang out with a book."

He left a tip on the table for the waitress and escorted Colin and Dylan out of the restaurant. When he'd suggested eating at Ruthie's he had not expected to see Jessica there. Waiting until both boys were seated and belted in, he started up the Jeep and maneuvered out of the crowded parking lot. He had come back to Wickham Falls to reconnect with his family, not to fall under the spell of a woman.

Chapter Four

Sawyer retrieved a visitor's pass from the front desk at the county hospital and took the elevator to the second floor. The numbers on the wall indicated his father's room was down the hallway on his right. He walked in and stopped when he saw a nurse at his father's bedside.

She glanced up and flashed a polite smile. "Could you please step outside, sir? I'll be finished in a few minutes."

He retreated, leaning against a wall in the immaculate wing dedicated to cardiac patients. Mara had returned to the house in good spirits because Henry had been moved out of ICU and into a semiprivate room. He'd barely had time to ask her about Henry's condition because Dylan and Colin regaled her excitedly with what they had eaten at Ruthie's.

The nurse stuck her head out the door. "Sir, you can

come in now. I had to change his IV and check his vitals."

"How is he? I'm his son," Sawyer explained when she gave him a questioning look.

"He's progressing well. You can get the name of his doctor from the nurse's station and he'll tell you everything."

"Thank you."

Sawyer entered the sun-filled room, his gaze fixed on the figure in the bed closest to the window. Sawyer didn't know what to expect when he glanced down at his father but it wasn't the man he hardly recognized. Henry Middleton was only sixty-seven yet appeared at least ten years older. As a former merchant seaman the elements had not been kind to his complexion. Streaks of silver were threaded between fading strawberry blonde curls.

Reaching for a chair, Sawyer pulled it closer to the bed and stared at Henry, who appeared to be sleeping. His chest rose and fell in an even rhythm. Sawyer ran his forefinger down the limp right hand resting on the snowy-white sheet, finding the skin cool to the touch. Then, without warning, Henry opened his eyes.

"You came." His voice was barely a whisper.

"Yes, Dad, I came."

Tears filled his red-rimmed blue eyes. "I prayed you'd come."

Sawyer felt a lump forming in his throat as he watched his father cry. Rachel said Henry had changed, but he never could have imagined the dictatorial man shedding even a single tear. He patted Henry's hand. "And your prayers are answered." Rising slightly, Sawyer reached for the box of tissues on the bedside table. He gently blotted Henry's cheeks. How was he to comfort a man who'd never shown him a modicum of gentleness, a man who preferred ridicule to compliments?

"How...long...long are you sta...ying?" Henry's eyelids fluttered.

"I'll be here until the end of summer." Sawyer wasn't certain if his father heard him, because he suspected the nurse had given him a sedative.

A hint of a smile parted the older man's lips. "I feel like an elephant's sitting on my chest." His smile faded as he closed his eyes again. "I guess I'm going to feel some pain for a while. Do you know they put stents in my arteries?"

"Yes, Dad, and you'll feel a lot better once you're out of here."

"When did you get here?"

"Yesterday."

"Who called you?"

"Rachel."

Henry chuckled softly. "I knew she would. It's good they brought me to her hospital so she can make certain they don't give me the wrong medication."

Sawyer shook his head. This was the Henry he knew. He hoped his father's brush with death had made him less negative. "They're not going to give you the wrong medication. And if you were going to die, then it would've happened before they got you to the hospital."

"I guess you're right."

"I know I'm right."

Henry breathed out a lingering sigh. "I remember you telling me that I'm too mean to die."

Sawyer nodded. "I seem to remember saying that more than once."

"Do you realize you're right? That I'm too mean to

die? At least, not yet." Henry sighed again. "I think I'm going to sleep now. Will you stay with me until I fall asleep?"

Leaning over, Sawyer pressed a kiss to his forehead. "Yes." Seconds later soft snoring filled the room. He caught movement out of the corner of his eye, and saw Rachel in the doorway. Smiling, she motioned him closer. He stood and approached her.

"Did you get the chance to talk to Dad?" she whispered.

"Yes."

"Did he growl at you?"

"He's in no condition to growl at anyone. How long do you think he's going to be here?"

"Probably another two days, barring complications. He almost coded in the ambulance. I spoke to his cardiologist earlier this morning and he says they're going to get him out of bed tomorrow because they want him ambulatory."

"Will he be able to walk stairs?"

"Not for at least a week. I'll have Mom turn the family room into a temporary bedroom. The love seat converts into a bed." Rachel glanced at her watch. "I'm on meal break, so I'm going to grab a bite then take a power nap before I go back on duty."

"Make certain you get some sleep before you drive home. You don't need to drive drowsy."

"I have to get the boys up in the morning because they tend to—"

"Don't worry about the boys, Rachel," Sawyer said, cutting her off. "I'll get them up and see that they get on the bus."

"You don't have to do that, Sawyer."

"I don't mind. You hang out here and get some rest before you get behind the wheel. Remember, you're a nurse, not Superwoman."

Rachel flashed a tender smile. "I'm so glad you're here."

Sawyer hugged her. "So am I." He stood in the doorway and watched her retreating back before returning to sit at his father's bedside. He had not lied to Rachel. It felt good to sleep under the roof in the house where he had been raised, and he knew it was just a matter of time before word got out that he was back in Wickham Falls.

Reaching for his cell phone, he sent a group text to his partners:

My father had angioplasty surgery. He came through okay. Plan to spend summer here.

Seconds later a response from Elena popped up on his screen.

Glad to know your dad is okay. We told the staff about the hiatus. It didn't go over well although they're being paid. They still want to come into the office.

Darius: I don't have a problem with them coming in. What about you, Saw?

Sawyer: I'm with you, Darius. Maybe they'll come up with something spectacular before we go public.

Elena: Word!

Sawyer laughed softly. It was on a rare occasion Elena used slang. Sawyer sent another message.

I'll check in later for updates.

Darius: Speaking of updates I finally popped the question. Last night I asked Chloe to move in with me and she went off like a mad woman claiming her parents didn't raise her to shack up with a man. This morning I took her to a jeweler and told her to pick out a ring. I must admit my woman has fabulous taste in jewelry.

Sawyer: Congrats! It's about time, brother. When are you tying the knot?

Darius: Easter week, and I want you and Thom to be my groomsmen. Chloe wants a destination wedding, so I'm seriously thinking of chartering a ship leaving out of New York for the wedding party and holding the ceremony and reception in Key West.

Sawyer: I'm in.

Elena: You're next, Sawyer.

Sawyer: Nah!! Right now I'm cool being a bachelor.

Elena: Yeah right. I'm willing to bet some pretty young country girl is going to catch your eye and you'll stop all that talk about being a cool bachelor. In case you don't realize it, you're still a country boy.

Sawyer: What's wrong with being a country boy?

Elena: Nothing. Don't forget Thom comes from a little town in Tennessee and I wouldn't trade him in if Brad Pitt walked through my door right this very minute.

Sawyer: This country boy is going to ring off now. You guys give your better halves my best.

He was still smiling when he slipped the phone into the pocket of his jeans. Little had Elena known that a pretty country girl *had* caught his eye but that's where it began and ended.

He wanted Jessica Calhoun, not as a wife or even a lover, but as a friend. He didn't want to get too involved with her and then, come summer's end, leave her to return to New York.

The doorbell rang, followed by Bootsy's strident barking, as Jessica descended the staircase. "I'm coming, baby boy." Logan had called to let her know he was coming over so they could get a jump on the grant proposal.

She opened the front door and within seconds Jessica scooped him up and held him tightly as the dog continued growling. "Sorry about that," she said in apology. "He's usually more welcoming."

Logan patted the small dog on the head. "Hey, Bootsy."

"Come on in. I printed out two copies of last year's grant application so we each will have a copy. We'll work at the table in the eating nook where we will have more room."

Logan sniffed the air. "Something smells good."

"I'm cooking for the week. Do you want anything to eat or drink?"

"No, thank you."

Jessica indicated where Logan should sit and then placed Bootsy in his crate in the mudroom. She returned to the kitchen and sat on the cushioned bench seat opposite Logan. "Have you set a wedding date?"

A mysterious smile played at the corners of his mouth. "Yes. Bastille Day."

"You're getting married July fourteenth?"

Logan affected a wide grin. *"Oui, mademoiselle."*

She smiled. "Congratulations! I'd love to be a fly on the wall and see everyone's expression at the school when you show up wearing a wedding band."

"That's not nice, Miss Calhoun," he chided.

"And you're not nice, Mister Mysterious," Jessica countered teasingly, "playing the footloose and fancy-free bachelor when you have a girlfriend waiting for you in France."

"Not quite, Jessica. I've never dated any of the women who work for the school district, and that's why there's been gossip about my love life. The same can be said about you."

"You're right," she confirmed. Although she'd dated one man for several months after moving to West Virginia, Jessica had a hard-and-fast rule not to date her coworkers. "Well, let's get into this monster and see what we can salvage or if we have to come up with new strategies to present to the committee."

They spent more than three hours going over pages of the proposal, deleting data they'd submitted the year before, while jotting down notes along the margins for possible consideration. "I think we're aiming too low,"

Jessica said, as she studied the section with the award bid request.

"You're kidding, aren't you?"

"No, I'm not. Think about it, Logan. Other school districts are being awarded millions, while we're only asking for less than half a mil. That may indicate our need isn't as great as other districts. Our demand is as great as Newark, New Jersey's, where they got a hundred million in grants from Facebook cofounder Mark Zuckerberg."

"You can't compare a city like Newark, which probably has a total population of at least a quarter of a million, to a town like Wickham Falls, where we struggle to maintain a population over four thousand, with half of them children."

"I still think we've been going at it from the wrong direction," Jessica argued softly. "It's not so much about asking for money as it is showing a specific need. If you don't mind, I'd like to ask a friend's brother who is into computers if he can offer some input. He's a graduate of Wickham Falls' schools, and as an alumnus his feedback may prove invaluable."

Logan leaned back, his gaze never wavering. "If he agrees then I don't see why we can't bring him on as an unpaid consultant."

Jessica gathered the pages with their notes, walked Logan to the door and then released Bootsy from the mudroom. She picked him up, cradling him to her chest. "Baby, you're going to have to learn not to show your teeth at Mama's company or they'll think you have no home training."

Bootsy wiggled for her to put him down and ran into the mudroom, where his lead and harness hung from a hook on the door. Jessica doubted he needed to go out but decided to indulge him. Reaching for the can of pepper spray, she tucked it into the pocket of her jeans and put on her pet's outside gear. At the last possible minute she picked up her cell phone and left the house.

The following weekend Jessica got up Saturday morning and set out patio furniture before she returned to the kitchen to prepare for food for the Memorial Day weekend get-together. While she had invited Sawyer to bring his nephews over for the backyard cookout, she had also extended the invitation to the families of her girls'-night-out colleagues, Abby, Beatrice, and Carly—who referred to themselves as the ABCs. She had also sent Rachel a text asking her to come if she wasn't scheduled to work.

The doorbell echoed throughout the house and seconds later Bootsy bounded into the kitchen barking loudly for her to follow him. "I'm coming, baby boy." She knew Bootsy would continue to bark until she went to see who or what had caught his attention.

Jessica opened the front door and her pulse skipped a beat before settling back to a normal rhythm. Sawyer stood on the porch with Rachel and his nephews. His deeply tanned face under the New York Yankees baseball cap indicated he had spent time in the sun since she last saw him. The added color illuminated eyes that reminded her of polished sapphires. Jessica still couldn't figure out what was it about her best friend's brother that made her feel tingly all over. She opened the door wider.

"Welcome!" Her voice had gone up an octave and

Rachel, carrying the picnic hamper, looked at her as if she had suddenly taken leave of her senses.

"Hello, Miss Calhoun," the boys said in unison.

"Can we play with Bootsy?" Dylan asked.

"Yes. But if he starts panting too hard, then please bring him inside." As if on cue, the puppy raced after the two boys as they headed for the rear of the house. "You didn't have to bring anything," she told Sawyer, who cradled a plastic crate filled with beer and soft drinks to his chest.

"Down here we're taught never to come to someone's home empty-handed."

Rachel set the hamper on the ladder-back chair in the entryway and then patted her brother's back. "Nice talk for someone wearing a Yankees cap."

"Come with me, Sawyer, and I'll show you where you can put your contraband."

He laughed loudly. "Damn! You ladies are cold."

"Sawyer! You're going to have to watch your language," Rachel admonished. "You keep swearing, and Dylan and Colin are going to end up with sewer mouths."

"Sorry about that, sis." He followed Jessica as she led the way around the house to an expansive patio area. "Something smells real good."

Jessica glanced at him over her shoulder. "I hope you brought your appetite because I'm smoking brisket, ribs and chicken. I have hot dogs, burgers and links for the kids." She pointed to a large tin tub filled with ice, bottles of beer and juice and cans of soda. "I think there's still some room in there for your...contribution."

Sawyer gave her a level look. "I thought it was contraband?"

She scrunched up her nose. "Did I say contraband and not contribution?"

"You can't blame it on a slip of the tongue, because you know damn well…I mean you know right well what you meant."

"Rachel's right. You're going to have to clean up your language because there're going to be a few kids here this afternoon."

"How many?"

"About six, and that includes your nephews."

Sawyer put bottles of beer and soda into the tub of icy water. "I suppose I spend too much time around adults."

"None of your friends in New York have children?"

"No." He stood straight, giving Jessica a long, penetrating stare, and realized she was a chameleon. The first time he'd seen her she was dressed to the nines, and then her clothes had been casual-chic at the restaurant, and now she appeared no older than a college coed with a white tank top, matching cropped pants and blue-and-white-striped espadrilles. She had covered her hair with a white bandana. And what Sawyer could not decide was which Jessica he liked best.

Sawyer's gaze swept over the patio that had an outdoor kitchen. "I've passed this house a few times but I never knew there was this much land behind it." He deliberately changed the topic from marriage and babies because he was tired of Rachel accusing him of being selfish because he wasn't willing to settle down. He had time to find that special woman with whom to share his life.

"It's a little more than an acre," Jessica said.

"What I do remember is the owners had their own garden and sold most of what they grew."

"The greenhouses are still here. They're hidden behind the trees, and they're the reason I bought this place."

His eyebrows lifted. "You're kidding."

"Nope. I grow all of my fruits, vegetables and flowers."

"The flowers you sent my father were from your garden?"

"Yes. Unfortunately I didn't get to see him when I went to the hospital because he was with his therapist at the time, so I just left them along with a card."

Folding his arms over his chest, Sawyer angled his head. Jessica was more an enigma than he had originally thought. Somehow he could not imagine a twenty-first-century thirty-something career woman farming. "I still can't believe you grow your own flowers and produce."

"The next time you come over I'll give you a tour."

"Will there be a next time?" he asked. He schooled his expression not to reveal the anticipation that Jessica would invite him to her home again.

"I'm certain there'll be."

Sawyer successfully hid a smile behind an expression of indifference. Jessica's offer for him to come back to her home was definitely a pleasant surprise and totally unexpected.

"Is there anything else I can do to help out before the others get here?"

"No. You're a guest, Sawyer."

"It's a backyard cookout, not a formal dinner, and if you've been up for hours putting all of this together then it means you'll probably be too tired to enjoy your *guests*. Now, please tell me how I can help you."

A slow smile softened her lips, drawing his gaze to linger there. "You're quite the silver-tongued devil when it comes to piling on the guilt."

Sawyer winked at her. "It's more like being persuasive."

Jessica rested a hand on his forearm. "Okay, Mister Persuasive. You can fire up the grill and cook burgers and hot dogs for the kids. They'll probably want to eat before the adults."

Rachel joined them on the patio. "Is there something I can do before the others get here?"

"You can help me set the table," Jessica told her. "All of the dishes and serving pieces are stacked on the kitchen countertop."

Sawyer cocked his head to one side. "I think I hear someone calling you, Jessica."

"You must have ears like a bat," Jessica teased as she turned and walked around the house.

Rachel stared at Sawyer's impassive expression. "You've really got it bad, brother love."

He frowned at Rachel. "What are you talking about?"

"Jessica. You really like her, don't you?"

He adjusted his cap and pulled it lower on his forehead. "What's there not to like? She's pretty, smart, and she seems to have charmed the pants off our family."

"That's not what I'm talking about, Sawyer. You like Jessica the way a man likes a woman."

"Do you want me to lie?"

"No. I'm glad you like her because I think she's good for you."

Sawyer walked to the gas grill and pushed buttons

to ignite the propane, his sister shadowing his steps. "Good how?"

"She has all the qualities you should look for in a woman who could become your potential wife."

Sawyer gave Rachel an incredulous stare. "When did you become a matchmaker? Because I've never had a problem letting a woman know I was interested in her. That's enough about me and Jessica. I've been assigned the task of manning the grill, so I need to get busy."

Chapter Five

Jessica greeted Carly Adams with a hug and an air kiss. Carly wore a straw hat to shield her fair skin from the intense late-spring sun as well as the ubiquitous blue-tinted glasses that protected her eyes, which were sensitive to bright light.

"I hope that tin you're holding is filled with your decadent chocolate chip cookies," Jessica said.

"Now, you know I wouldn't come without them," Carly confirmed.

"Bless you, my child." Jessica loved cooking, but drew the line at desserts because they involved too many steps and ingredients. The first time she'd tasted Carly's chocolate chip cookies, though, she was addicted.

"Where are your children?" Jessica asked as they walked around the house to the patio.

"Benny's bringing them later. Katie had a sleepover and he went to get her. Are you holding out on us again?" Carly whispered when she spied Sawyer at the grill.

"What are you talking about?" Jessica asked.

"The delicious-looking man at the grill. You know it's all over the school that you and Logan Fowler are together."

Jessica cut her eyes at her friend. "You know Logan and I are on the same committee, and I'd never date a colleague. By the way, Sawyer is the uncle of the Phelan twins and my best friend's brother. Now, stop gawking and come with me. I'll introduce you to him." She bit back a smile. Sawyer had removed his cap and fashioned his hair into a bun.

Jessica introduced Carly to Sawyer then repeated the action when Abby and Beatrice arrived with their families. She found it hard to conceal her amusement as the two women appeared to be quite taken with Rachel's brother; he morphed into the quintessential Southern gentleman, bowing slightly and kissing the backs of their hands, and greeting their husbands with strong hugs. Carly's husband and children arrived at the same time Dylan and Colin returned from romping with Bootsy, and her son and daughter joined the other tweens when they gathered on the porch and in the hammock with their electronic gadgets.

Jessica went into the kitchen to fill a large straw basket with an assortment of condiments. Her holiday menu also included spicy coleslaw, baked beans, corn on the cob and a garden salad with chickpeas tossed with vinaigrette to go along with the smoked brisket, ribs and chicken. Beatrice and Abby brought a fruit salad and miniature red-velvet cupcakes. Sawyer appeared right at home as he alternated flipping burgers with drinking beer while he and the men, also claiming their own beers, carried on lively conversations about various sports teams.

"It looks as if Sawyer has found himself a few new buddies," Jessica said to Rachel.

Rachel laughed softly. "Give a man a beer and put him in charge of a grill and he's in heaven. Add a few buddies and it's nirvana. I'm willing to bet that he'll be hanging out with Abby's and Beatrice's husbands at the Wolf Den, debating how they can solve the world's problems. I'll have to reserve judgment for Carly's snobby better half. I'm even surprised he came here today."

"Maybe some of Carly's liberalism is rubbing off on him. We'll just have to wait and see if he attempts to step foot into Wickham Fall's legendary sports bar." A few times she had driven along the road not far from the Wolf Den but she'd never stopped in, even though they were purported to serve the best steak sandwiches in the county, if not the entire state.

Rachel wrinkled her nose. "I used to go there with Mason, but somehow I was never fascinated with a place where all I could smell is beer. By the way, you really outdid yourself today with all this food," she said, complimenting Jessica.

"It's really not that much. I've put aside some low-fat, salt-free dishes for your father." Rachel had revealed her mother spent most of her free time taking her husband to rehab and seeing to Henry's immediate needs.

"Mom will really appreciate that. She knows Dad has to watch his diet, so she ignores him when he complains about not being able to eat fried foods."

"He'll get used to a different diet after a while." Jessica went completely still when she detected the scent of Sawyer's cologne as he came up behind her.

"I don't know how you like your burger. Try this one and let me know."

Turning slowly, she glanced up at him. "I usually like mine medium-well." Holding on to his wrist she bit into the hamburger, savoring the piquant taste of pepper jack cheese and minced onions stuffed inside lean sirloin on a potato roll. "Wow," she crooned. He'd cooked it just the way she liked. "That's really good." She was just about to take another bite when Sawyer took a big mouthful.

Nodding, he slowly chewed at the same time he closed his eyes. "You're right. It is good."

He held the burger above his head when she reached for it. "Hey, that's mine!"

"I'll bring you another one," Sawyer promised as he popped what remained into his mouth. "The cook needs to know if the chef approves of his skills."

"I approve," she said. A smile crinkled the skin around her eyes as she went to the smoker to check on the meat.

Later that night, after everyone had left, Jessica shifted in the hammock. The lingering aroma of grilling meats wafted in the nighttime air. She closed her eyes. Citronella candles were sputtering and burning out along with a dozen pillars in wrought-iron lanterns ringing the patio; she knew it was just a matter of time before swarms of mosquitos would use her exposed skin for a meal.

She must have drifted off to sleep because the ringing of the house phone along with Bootsy's barking jolted Jessica awake. Crawling out of the hammock, she opened the French doors and walked into the kitchen. It was only on a rare occasion her landline rang, and she assumed at that hour it had to be one of her parents. She stared at the caller ID: Henry Middleton. She whispered a silent prayer that it wasn't bad news—that Henry had not suffered a setback.

Jessica picked up the receiver. "Hello."

"Jessica, this is Sawyer. I'm sorry to be calling so late, but Rachel can't find her cell phone and she thinks she left it at your place."

"Let me check outside and I'll call you back."

"That's all right. I'll hang on."

Jessica set the receiver on the countertop and returned to the patio. She checked the tables and then seat cushions. Wedged between a lounge chair cushion was a wristlet. Inside the small purse was a cell phone. She went back into the house and picked up the handset. "I found it. I'll bring it over."

"Don't bother. I'm coming to get it."

"But I don't..." Her words trailed off. Sawyer had hung up on her.

Ten minutes later she heard the sound of an approaching vehicle, and when she stepped outside the house under the gabled entrance she saw Sawyer getting out of an SUV. He covered a yawn with his hand. Walking down two steps, she met him as he came up the path.

"Here you are, sleepyhead," she teased, handing him the wristlet.

"Sorry about that."

Jessica tried making out his features in the shrouded

darkness. "Would you like some coffee before you drive back?"

His teeth shone whitely in his tanned face. "That sounds like an offer I can't refuse." He patted Bootsy's head when the dog came over to sniff him and followed Jessica as she went back into the house. "I lecture Rachel about driving drowsy and right now I'm the guilty one."

"Working the graveyard shift can do that to her," Jessica said over her shoulder.

Sawyer stared at the gentle sway of Jessica's hips, and wondered if she was totally oblivious to the innate femininity that threatened to send his libido into overdrive. There had been a time when Rachel accused him of dating airheads, and when he compared them to Jessica he had to admit Rachel wasn't that far off. Aside from their overall attractiveness, some of his dates had been dull and self-centered.

His gaze swept over the furnishings in the entryway, living and dining rooms as he walked into the kitchen. The layout of the first floor provided a sense of openness because the rooms were decorated using a minimalist design, and he wondered if Jessica had employed the services of a professional decorator.

"You can tell you don't have any children."

"Why do you say that?" Jessica asked.

"Your house is spotless." The pale walls were pristine and gleaming parquet floors were covered with beautiful area rugs.

Turning, she met his eyes. "I'm a little anal when it comes to keeping a clean house."

He gave her a questioning look. "A little?"

"Okay. I'll admit I'm a neat freak. But that's not to say that if I ever have children I'd go behind them with a broom or a cloth wiping away spills. Children need freedom to explore and feel comfortable in their environment."

Sawyer leaned against the entrance to the kitchen and watched Jessica as she washed her hands in a sink at the cooking island. He studied her every move as she took down a mug from an overhead cabinet. "Do you want children?" The question had come out unbidden.

Jessica went completely still, and then she recovered. "I have children. Fifteen to be exact."

He approached Jessica. His height advantage allowed him to see the carefully layered strands covering her head. "I meant children of your own."

"If I decide I want children then I'll consider adoption." She turned on the single cup coffeemaker. "Regular or decaf?"

"Regular." She plucked a pod off the coffee carousel and slipped it into the well.

"What about you, Sawyer? Do you plan to marry and have children?"

Damn, he thought. While he was probing into her life she'd suddenly turned the tables on him. "Maybe one of these days."

"So you're not antimarriage?"

He angled his head. "Not in the least. I'm just not ready to settle down with a wife at this time in my life."

A beat passed as Sawyer recalled many of the lectures he'd had from his father. While he had not agreed with Henry's method of child-rearing, he did respect his father when he preached to him that he had to be responsible—that his actions always had consequences. If he slept with a woman without using protection and she became pregnant, then he had to do the right thing and take care of her and the child. And for Henry, the right thing was marrying her.

Jessica pulled down the lever and punched the button to start the brewing cycle. "I have more students than I care to count who're being raised by single mothers while their fathers aren't remotely in their lives."

"Like Rachel?"

"No, Sawyer. Not like Rachel. Dylan and Colin know who their father is, while these children have never set eyes on their fathers. Not all couples can stay together, but that doesn't excuse parents for not putting aside their differences for the sake of their children."

"You talk about single mothers. What about single fathers?"

"I've had a few of them. There are times when I'm more social worker than teacher when confronted with problems that are outside my role as an educator."

"What do you do?"

"I refer them to the school psychologist. Do you want milk or cream?" she asked when the brewing cycle ended.

"I'll drink it black." He took the mug from her. "Aren't you going to join me?"

Jessica shook her head. "My quota is one cup in the morning. If I drink coffee at night I have trouble falling asleep. I've tried decaf and the result is the same."

Sawyer wanted to tell Jessica he had a surefire way of assuring her of a restful night's sleep, but it included sharing a bed. He walked over to the eating nook and waited for her to sit before he sat opposite her. His eyes swept around the ultramodern stainless-steel kitchen. Shiny copper pots and pans were suspended on a rack above the cooking island and a variety of herbs grew in small hand-painted flowerpots lining the ledge of the boxed bay window.

"How much work did you put into this house?" It was safer to broach a generic topic than to think about wanting to make love to Jessica. She was the first woman in a very long time to whom he had found himself physically attracted on sight and that made him slightly off balance when around Jessica.

Jessica didn't want to believe she was sitting across the table in her kitchen talking to a man who made her feel incredibly comfortable in his presence. She found herself physically attracted to Sawyer and that, in and of itself, shocked her, because it had been a long time since she felt desire that palpable. Sawyer was so quintessentially masculine it radiated off him in waves. There were times she detected something in his eyes that she believed meant he could read her thoughts but she dismissed it as mere curiosity. It would stand to reason that he was curious about his sister's best friend and his nephews' former teacher.

"An engineer deemed the house structurally sound, and that meant I only had to concentrate on the interior. The contractor removed walls for an open floor plan, installed new windows with built-in mini-blinds and replaced the siding and roof. He updated the downstairs half-bath, gutted the kitchen and put in French doors leading to the back porch, so I have light here from sunrise to sunset."

"How many bathrooms do you have upstairs?"

"Two."

Sawyer sipped the hot liquid. "Who decorated your home?"

"I did. The smoker belonged to my great-grandfather, who'd earned the reputation of being Pittsburgh's best grill master when it came to smoking brisket and ribs."

His expression brightened. "So, you're from Steel City."

Guilty as charged. "Steelers, Pirates, Penguins and anything black-and-gold."

"You're really that into sports?"

"Only if the home teams are playing."

Sawyer took another swallow of coffee. "Have you been to the Wolf Den to watch your teams?"

"No."

"Would you like to go there with me?"

Jessica smiled. "Are you asking me out?"

"Yes."

She paused. She hadn't dated in two years and now her best friend's brother wanted her to go out with him. Jessica liked Sawyer—a lot.

"Okay," she said after a noticeable pause.

His eyebrows lifted. "Is that a yes?"

She nodded. "It is a yes."

Sawyer smiled and exhaled an audible breath. "What made you leave Pittsburgh for West Virginia?"

She knew she had to choose her words carefully or disclose the actual reason that had forced her to leave the city of her birth and never look back.

"College." It was a half-truth. Jessica told Sawyer that she attended Howard University in DC, and after graduating had taught in a local elementary school while earning a graduate degree. "I went online and discovered Johnson County public schools in West Virginia were looking for teachers. I submitted my résumé and after a couple of interviews they hired me. Relocating wasn't a problem because I was renting."

"That's when you moved to Beckley."

"Yes. I rented a studio apartment that was so small I felt claustrophobic. And I didn't like the idea of cooking and sleeping in the same space."

"I would've prayed for a studio just to have some personal space, because it has to be better than sharing a one-bedroom apartment with three dudes."

Propping an elbow on the table, Jessica rested her chin on the heel of her hand. "When did you do that?"

Sawyer set his mug on the table. "I'd enrolled in NYU as a grad student and finding an apartment I could afford without having to sell a kidney was virtually impossible, so I hooked up with four guys to share a one-bedroom apartment in a neighborhood known as Alphabet City. It meant three weeks out of the month it was either sleeping on the convertible sofa or on the floor in a sleeping bag. Most times I opted for my sleeping bag."

"That's cruel and unusual punishment."

"No shit! Sorry about that," he apologized quickly.

Jessica giggled like her students whenever they found something laughable. "Your New York is showing."

Sawyer sobered. "What do you know about New York?"

She wanted to tell him there was no need to sound so defensive about his adopted city. Her Howard University roommate grew up in New York. "The proliferation of colorful language. And I know enough not to play chicken with New York City cabbies, or close my eyes when riding the subway."

"Whoa! Why are you dissing my city?"

"I'm not dissing your city, Sawyer. I'm just being truthful. The same could be said for Philly, LA or even DC."

He flashed a saccharine smile. "Is Pittsburgh included in that mix?"

She lifted her shoulders. "Could be." Jessica loved her city of birth because her familial roots were ingrained in the city's steel industry. She had planned to spend all of her life in Pittsburgh, but an incident at college had forced her to leave. After witnessing the rape of her roommate by a popular football player, the backlash she encountered from her fiancé and fellow students after she reported the incident to campus officials devastated her and resulted in her transferring to another college out of state. Not only had Gregory ended their engagement, he had also sided with those at their college who supported the college's quarterback, who'd claimed the sex was consensual.

"Why did you become a teacher?"

"Teaching is a family tradition. My parents recently retired as college professors, and I told you about my grandmother. I want to thank you for getting the men to clean up," she segued smoothly, shifting the focus from herself to Sawyer. Whenever she invited her friends over it was the women who assumed the task of clearing away dishes and leftovers.

Sawyer slid off the seat, walked to the sink, rinsed the mug and placed it in the dishwasher. "If you cooked, the least we could do was clean up. Thanks for the coffee." Reaching for her hand, he laced their fingers together. "Walk with me to the door."

Jessica detected calluses on his palm that indicated Sawyer was no stranger to manual labor. His roughened hand was totally incongruent with someone who earned his living sitting at a desk.

"Are you alert enough to make it back home okay?"

He gave her fingers a gentle squeeze. "I'm good. Thank you again for your wonderful hospitality." He shocked her completely when he released her hand and angled his head to brush a kiss over her mouth. She went completely still for several seconds and then relaxed as her lips parted. The touch of his mouth on hers was a reminder for Jessica that it had been much too long since a man had kissed her. "Once the school year ends I'll call you about going to the Wolf Den. Good night, Jessica."

Although the kiss could be measured in fractions of seconds, the taste of coffee from his lips lingered on hers. "Good night, Sawyer." Jessica stood on the steps with Bootsy as Sawyer started up the Jeep and reversed. When she had offered him a cup of coffee, she never expected that he would ask her out or that she would accept. He waved through the open driver's-side window and she returned it, smiling. Bootsy growled softly. "I know, boy. I'll take you for your last walk before I lock up."

Forty minutes later she stepped out of the shower, toweled dry her body and slipped a nightgown over her head. She fell asleep as soon as her head touched the pillow. Hours later a dream jolted her into wakefulness as her heart pounded a runaway rhythm. Sitting up, Jessica peered at the clock on the bedside table. It was after three in the morning. She had dreamed of her brother.

Marine helicopter pilot Captain Elliot Calhoun loved red roses and he confided to her he always recited a psalm before lifting off; the ritual ended when his copter was shot down by a rocket-propelled grenade during a rescue mission.

It was after four when she fell asleep again, and when she woke hours later the sun was high in the sky. Bootsy lay on the rug beside her bed, muzzle resting between his paws, waiting for her to get up and let him out.

Chapter Six

"Put your arms around my neck, Dad. That way it will be easier for me to lift you."

Henry shook his head. "Let me get down by myself. I'm too heavy for you to carry."

Sawyer closed his eyes for several seconds. "I'm not going to let you get down by yourself. If you fall you'll be back in the hospital. What's it going to be, Dad?"

Henry grunted. "Okay. But just this one time."

Much too stubborn to acknowledge when he had been bested, Henry looped both arms around his son's neck and Sawyer easily carried him from the car, into the house and to the family room, where Mara had converted the sofa into a bed. He set his father down on a leather recliner, elevating the footrest and then smoothed graying wisps off Henry's cool forehead. He'd driven his father to rehab earlier that morning, but the therapist canceled the session when Henry complained of feeling light-headed.

Henry pointed to the wall-mounted flat screen. "Son, can you please turn on the TV? I like watching the cooking channels."

Reaching for the remote, Sawyer turned on the television, surfing until he found one of the many channels devoted to food. "I'm going to bring in the walker and leave it close to your chair in case you need to use the bathroom."

"I don't need the walker," Henry countered. "I've been using the cane."

"I'll leave it here if you decide you do need it."

"I said I don't need it!" Henry shouted.

Sawyer returned to the porch to get the walker. Henry gave Sawyer what he interpreted as a death stare when he returned and placed the walker next to the recliner and then picked up the quad cane and put it out of the older man's reach. In the past he would have verbally come back at his father. But, given Henry's medical condition, Sawyer decided action outweighed words.

Mara entered the room carrying a lap tray. "Why did you bring in the walker?"

Sawyer met his father's eyes. "Your husband has been complaining that he feels light-headed, so the walker is better for him right now than the cane."

"I'm better now," Henry said, frowning. "And I don't enjoy being treated like a child." He pointed at Sawyer. "That was the first and last time I'm going to let you carry me."

Folding his arms over his chest, Sawyer gave him a direct stare. "Would you prefer if I had to pick you off the floor?"

Mara placed the tray on a low table in front of the love seat. "Please don't start up with him, Sawyer. And stop complaining, Henry, and eat your lunch. I made broiled chicken, steamed carrots and sliced avocado."

Henry gave her a tender smile. "Thank you. It looks delicious. I'd prefer fried chicken but I suppose this will have to do."

Mara wagged her finger. "No more fried food until you get your cholesterol under control."

"Are you going to eat with me, hon?"

"Do you want me to?" Mara asked.

"Yes, please."

Sawyer shared a glance with Mara. She'd told him Henry had changed, and except for the protestations when he attempted to assist his father from the Jeep and Henry's reluctance to use the walker rather than the cane, Sawyer realized she was right. Henry rarely referred to him as *son* and hardly ever said please or thank-you.

"Are you going to eat with us, Sawyer?" Henry questioned.

"No, Dad. I have to go to Grand's Hardware to buy some paint and tape."

"You did a nice job fixing the porch. But then, you were always good with your hands."

Sawyer had removed the shutters and replaced the sagging floor boards on the porch. "That's because I learned from the best." Sawyer executed a snappy salute. "I'll see you later."

He knew he'd shocked his father with the compliment. Whenever Henry came home on an extended shore leave he would spend the time making repairs around the house, and once Sawyer was old enough,

Henry recruited him as his assistant. By the time he turned sixteen, Sawyer was able to repair a car's engine and measure and cut wood with enough precision to fit floor joists. His father was a hard taskmaster and most times he bit his tongue rather than argue with the older man, but as he got older he'd felt compelled to challenge his father.

Sawyer knew their roles had changed to where he hoped they would be able to relate to each other as adult men. He respected Henry because he was his father, yet knew it would take time to respect him as a man.

He had asked his mother what color she wanted him to paint the shutters and porch floor to contrast with the house's white vinyl siding. Mara had suggested blue, and after he'd picked up a number of paint swatches in varying shades of blue from the local hardware store, she finally settled on Wedgewood blue.

Sawyer slowed to less than ten miles an hour when he entered the business district. Long-time residents were programmed not to drive above the unofficial twenty miles an hour in fear of the escalating exorbitant traffic fines imposed by the members of the town council.

Wickham's Main Street appeared to have been stuck in time, with the exception of new black-and-white-striped awnings shading mom-and-pop-owned stores. Cars, parked diagonally, maximized the limited space along the narrow streets. Shop Local signs were visible on every plate-glass window. Many of the stores had been owned by generations of the same family, and most residents of Wickham didn't have to leave their town for clothes, banking, medical assistance or eating establishments.

Sawyer maneuvered into a parking space behind the hardware store. A cowbell over the rear screen door clanged loudly as he walked in. He picked up a roll of yellow tape, his thoughts dwelling on Jessica as he waited for the salesclerk to mix the colors for his paint selection. He had deliberately kept busy making repairs on the house so he would not think about her.

Not only was she an incredible cook but she was the consummate hostess, and in a moment of madness Sawyer fantasized being married to Jessica and hosting get-togethers for their friends and family. As soon as the notion entered his head he dismissed it. He wasn't ready for marriage and he did not want to spend the rest of his life living in a small town.

"Do you need brushes, turpentine or drop cloths, Sawyer?"

He stared at Johnnie Lee Grand.

"No thank you, Mr. Grand. I just need the paint and the tape."

Johnnie rang up Sawyer's purchases. "I heard about your father. How's he doing?"

"Much better, thank you. He's going to have to take it easy for a while."

"Give him my best."

"I will."

Sawyer left the store and drove home. He became a sightseer in his home state, his gaze taking in the forest-covered mountains in the distance. Wickham Falls lay in a region where coal mining and drilling for natural gas provided many of the residents with employment.

Sawyer arrived home and decided to paint the shutters first. He spread out three oversized drop cloths on the grass under the shade of two towering oak trees, filled a paint gun and began the task of covering eighteen pairs of shutters with high-gloss, quick-drying blue paint.

Jessica stood at the desk in her silent classroom. The school year had ended at noon and she could finally exhale. No more regimented days for laundry, ironing or cooking. She gave her students gift bags filled with grade-appropriate chapter books, colorful bookmarks, find-the-word puzzle workbooks and a journal for them to record their summer adventures. The faculty had their own end-of-the-year luncheon celebration when they ordered foot-long meat-and-veggie-stuffed heroes and salads from Ruthie's.

She took one last glance around and picked up her tote. A week before she had received official notification that she would teach fifth grade for the first time.

Fifth grade was middle school, which meant she would be teaching the same students she had taught three years before, and that meant the Phelan twins would become her students again.

Jessica parked on the street in front of the Middleton house. She had spent the afternoon weeding her garden and harvesting romaine lettuce, radicchio, scallions, green cabbage, tomatoes, cucumbers and red, yellow and green sweet peppers. It would be several more weeks before the melons ripened enough for her to pick them. The prior owners had sold their yield, while Jessica opted to give away all she wasn't able to consume or can. Two of her neighbors and the Middletons had become the recipients of her bounty.

Reaching for the shopping bag on the passenger seat, she alighted from the SUV. The glossy blue paint on the porch caught her immediate attention before her gaze shifted to the matching shutters. The color was a perfect match for the blue and white cushions on white wicker porch furniture. The inner wooden door, also painted the same hue and bearing a new brass knocker and doorknob, was open. Jessica peered through the screen door while Sawyer stood on the other side staring at her. His now-familiar masculine cologne wafted to her nostrils as he opened the door.

"Hey," he crooned.

"Hey, yourself," she countered. "I came over to bring some veggies from my garden." Jessica handed him the shopping bag.

He reached for her hand, dropping a kiss on her fingers. "Don't leave," he said softly when she turned to retrace her steps. "Have you had dinner?" He smiled and attractive lines fanned out around his luminous eyes.

"No."

Sawyer leaned in closer, his moist breath feathering over her ear. "It's taco night at the Middletons', and I might sound a little biased, but my mother makes the best tacos and nachos I've ever eaten. Besides, my dad will be glad to see you." He pulled her gently inside the house.

"The porch and the shutters look nice." Jessica had to say something—anything—because just being close to Sawyer and his holding her hand made her insides quiver like gelatin. Everything about him turned her on, including his voice with just a hint of a Southern cadence. She did not want to think of his tall, slender body without an ounce of excess fat. It had been a long time since she'd felt physically attracted to a man, and even longer since she had slept with one.

"They look nice because my dear brother painted them." Rachel had overheard her compliment.

Jessica met Sawyer's eyes. "Please don't tell me you climbed up on a ladder to paint them."

Bringing her hand to his mouth, he dropped another kiss on her knuckles. "I didn't know you cared."

She tried extricating her hand but he tightened his grip. His hold, although firm, wasn't enough to cause her pain or discomfort. "Your family has been through enough with your father, and if you were foolish enough to go up on a ladder and fall off and crack your noggin, then you'd deserve it."

"Those are harsh words coming from a school-marm."

"Stop teasing her, Sawyer," Rachel chastised, cutting her eyes at him. "Sometime my brother has a weird sense of humor. Jessica, I hope you're staying for dinner. It's taco night."

"Sawyer already invited me."

"Good." Rachel forcibly pulled Jessica away from Sawyer. "Let go of her." Sawyer released Jessica's hand. "You'll have all summer to see her now that she's not going to visit her folks in Seattle."

Jessica stared at Rachel then Sawyer, wondering if she was missing something. Had the siblings discussed her in depth? And what had been Sawyer's response? Was that why he'd asked her out?

She wrested the shopping bag from his other hand.

"Excuse me, but I have to see if your mother needs help in the kitchen."

Sawyer had not moved. It had taken all of his self-control not to gawk at the outline of Jessica's full breasts under her white T-shirt.

"I warned you before not to play with her."

He frowned at his sister. "Mind your business, Rachel." He didn't bother to hide his annoyance at her meddling.

Rachel took a step, bringing them within a hairsbreadth of each other. "Jessica is my business, because I don't want you to take advantage of her."

Pulling her close, Sawyer pressed his mouth to his sister's ear. "Jessica is more than capable of taking care of herself. And she doesn't need you to be her mouthpiece. And she's already agreed to go with me to the Wolf Den. Jessica would not be the first woman I've dated and not slept with, so get your mind out of the gutter, dear sister."

Rachel eased back. "You're kidding, aren't you?"

Sawyer wanted to ask his sister if she thought he was such a monster he would force a woman to sleep with him. Although he had a very healthy libido, there were periods when he was celibate and always by choice. He equated sharing a woman's bed with emotional involvement and there were liaisons he ended before finding himself in too deep. Draping an arm over Rachel's shoulders he steered her through the living room and into the kitchen.

The sound of childish laughter came from the family room and he knew Colin, Dylan and their grandfather were watching cartoons. Henry's rapid convalescence far exceeded his doctor's treatment plan, and he had stopped complaining about his low-fat diet. After dinner his parents usually went for a walk, during which Henry monitored the number of steps he took on the pedometer strapped to his upper arm. They still had not had their heart-to-heart father-son talk and Sawyer did not want to be the one to initiate it.

Seeing his mother, sister and the woman with whom he had become entranced together was an image he would remember for a long time. Rachel and Jessica were gyrating to a popular dance hit. Mara, laughing uncontrollably, attempted to do the stanky leg.

Sawyer had synched Rachel's smartphone playlist with the speakers he had installed in the ceilings of the kitchen and family room. Pulling his cell phone out of the back pocket of his jeans, he videotaped his mother and sister. Mara saw him and an expression of shock froze her features as she went completely still.

"If you put this on the internet I'll disown you," Mara threatened, as he continued taping.

"Not to worry, Mom. Whenever I need a chuckle I'll replay this." Sawyer had to admit Jessica was a better than average dancer. When the song ended, he applauded.

Rachel wrinkled her nose at him. "Don't hate, brother, because you have two left feet"

He set the phone on the countertop. "No comment."

"You don't dance?" Jessica questioned.

Sawyer detected a hint of facetiousness in Jessica's query. "I slow dance." His sister was partially right about his not catching on to dances trending at clubs, but he did have rhythm. He leaned against the countertop and folded his arms over his chest. "Do you guys need my help?"

Mara shook her head. "We have everything under control here. Thanks to Jessica bringing over some peppers, I'll add fajitas to the menu."

He snapped his fingers, pantomiming castanets. "Olé!"

Sawyer left the kitchen, whistling a nameless tune as he strode into the family room. Colin and Dylan, flanking their grandfather on the sofa, laughed hysterically at the antics of an animated character. Henry acknowledged him with a smile, shifted his attention back to the television and laughed along with his grandsons.

Healthy color had returned to Henry's face and even his hair appeared fuller and shinier. Sawyer dropped down to a club chair, stretching out long legs and crossing them at the ankles. How different the relationship was between Henry and his grandchildren than it had been with Sawyer when he was their age. Although his father was away eight out of twelve months of the year, his homecomings had been viewed with trepidation. Henry's unwritten mantra had been *either my way or the highway*. Whenever Henry issued a command he expected everyone not to challenge or question his authority, and that included his wife. And because he felt helpless when it came to dealing with his father, Sawyer had begun talking back. Henry retaliated by grounding him. Sawyer stayed in his room, reading and listening to music. The year he turned thirteen his mother had bought him a personal computer, which changed his life. He took every available computer course in high school and specialized in computer science while in the military.

He had just turned eighteen when he'd had a volatile confrontation with his father that could have become physical if Sawyer hadn't walked away. The next day he'd sought out the army recruiter who had come to the high school and made a commitment to join once he graduated. It had taken years of separation and talking to an army psychologist for Sawyer to acknowledge Henry's need to always be in control. Slumping lower in the chair, Sawyer sat watching the screen until Rachel announced it was time to eat.

Chapter Seven

Jessica sat across the table from Sawyer, their eyes meeting each time she glanced up. Taco night included guacamole, pork carnitas tacos, nachos with baked corn chips, shredded slow-cooked chicken infused with orange juice, melted cheddar and pepper jack cheeses, and black bean salsa.

Henry held up his flour tortilla–wrapped chicken fajita. "This is good stuff. Thanks, honey."

Mara raised her glass of lemonade in acknowledgment. "Thank Jessica."

"I don't mind eating vegetables but a man needs to sink his teeth into some meat every once in a while. Right, Sawyer?"

Sawyer lifted his glass of sweet tea in confirmation. "Right, Dad. I tried going vegetarian for a month, and by the third week I caved when I went to a steak house and ordered the biggest steak they had."

"Did you finish it, Uncle Sawyer?" Dylan asked.

"I couldn't. It was just too much to eat in one sitting."

Mara tucked a strand of silver-streaked dark hair behind one ear as she trained blue-gray eyes on Jessica. "Have you ever been to New York?"

Jessica set down her fork. "I've been there twice."

"Did you like it?" Rachel questioned.

"I did."

Rachel refilled her glass from the pitcher of cranberry juice. "I don't think I'd be able to adjust to living in a city with millions of people and bumper-to-bumper traffic."

"You forget, I come from a big city. Pittsburgh can't compare to New York City when it comes to population, but they don't roll up the streets at night like here in Wickham Falls."

"So, you like living here?" Mara asked her.

"I love living here. Right now I couldn't see myself living anywhere else."

"I wish my son felt the same as you," Mara mumbled under her breath.

Jessica saw Sawyer's expression change from amusement to annoyance. His mouth tightened noticeably as he dropped his gaze. "Not now, Mom."

"Did I say something wrong?" Mara appeared to be the poster child for unadulterated innocence.

"Mara, honey," Henry said in a quiet voice. "Please let it go. Sawyer is a grown man who can live anywhere he wants."

"But—"

Henry stared at his wife. "We'll talk about this later."

Jessica shifted uneasily in her chair. She felt like a spy, eavesdropping on a conversation that had nothing to do with her. She was more than aware that all families had disagreements. An uncomfortable silence followed as everyone focused on their plates.

Rachel dabbed her mouth, then placed her napkin beside her plate. "Sawyer, could you please turn on the computer for Colin and Dylan? Now, please," she added when he hesitated. He pushed back his chair, stood up and walked out of the dining room. Dylan and Colin raced after him.

Jessica knew it was time to take her leave because she was becoming more uncomfortable with each passing minute. "Thank you for dinner. It was delicious."

"You can't leave until you have dessert," Mara said. "I made caramel flan."

"Mom, please don't get up until Sawyer gets back," Rachel said softly. "I want you all to hear what I have to say."

"Even me?" Jessica asked.

"Even you, Jessica. You should know by now that we think of you as family."

Because her parents lived three thousand miles away, there were times when Jessica regarded the Middletons as her surrogate family. "It's the same with me and you guys," she said.

Sawyer returned to the table, this time sitting in the chair Colin had vacated, and draped an arm over Jessica's shoulders. "What do you want to say that you didn't want the boys to hear?"

"Mason wants the boys to spend their summer vacation with him."

Mara sat straight. "When did he tell you this?"

"In Hawaii?" Henry asked, not giving Rachel the chance to answer her mother's question.

"He called me earlier today. And, yes, in Hawaii.

Actually, he lives on the island of Oahu." She exhaled a sigh. "I may as well tell it all."

Sawyer leaned forward. "Please do."

Jessica listened along with the others as Rachel revealed her ex-husband had finally found success as a commercial artist. He had formèd a partnership with the son of a local hotel owner willing to invest in his business designing personal, one-of-a-kind surf-, skate- and snowboards for professionals. "People on the Big Island are calling him the Andy Warhol of surfboards."

"How long has he been designing them?" Sawyer asked.

"About eighteen months. He closed on a four-bedroom house last week and deposited enough money in my account to cover back child support payments and his payments for the rest of the year."

Henry ran a hand over his face. "Are you going to send them? Why now, Rachel, when he hasn't seen his sons in years?"

Rachel shook her head. "I can't answer why now. What bothers me is he's been more of a stranger than a father."

"You want us to help you make a decision?" Sawyer asked his sister.

Rachel affected a half smile. "Yes. Jessica, if you were in my situation would you let your children fly across the country to spend time with a man they hadn't seen in years?"

No, I wouldn't! Jessica's inner voice screamed. Why had Rachel put her on the spot when she didn't have children or an ex-husband? "No. If they go, then I would have to be with them."

"There you go, Rachel," Sawyer said. "You have your

answer. Tell Mason you and the kids are a package deal. After all, you're the custodial parent."

Rachel flashed a two-hundred-watt smile. "You're right, Sawyer. And thank you, Jess."

A slight frown creased Mara's forehead. "So, you're going?"

"I'm still thinking about it."

Henry cleared his throat. "When do you have to let him know?"

"There's no time limit. If I'm going, then I'll have to put in for vacation. I may have a problem because we're short-staffed in pediatrics."

Mara slammed her palm on the table, rattling plates and place settings. "If that hospital won't give you time off, then quit. You can always find another position at a hospital closer to home. Every time they need someone to fill in because a nurse is either on vacation or sick, you step up. You don't see yourself when you come home, dog-tired from working doubles. I'm not in favor of you taking up with Mason again because of how he deserted you, but I know you have to think of your children. And what you don't want is for your sons to blame you for not giving them the opportunity to get to know their father."

"You do look like crap," Henry said.

"You need a vacation, Rachel," Mara continued, as if her husband had not spoken. "And it doesn't matter whether it's here or in Hawaii. You—"

"I hear you, Mom," Rachel interrupted. "I'm going to give myself the weekend to think it over before I call Mason with an answer."

Jessica suspected Rachel had already made her decision. She also assumed the Middletons were not fond of the man who had deserted his wife and children to follow his dream; however, none had openly voiced their objection to Dylan and Colin reconnecting with their father.

Mara pressed her palms together. "I guess that settles that for now. Who's ready for dessert?"

Sawyer watched Jessica hug his mother, sister and father as she prepared to leave.

He took her hand. "I'll walk you to your car."

"I think I can find it without too much difficulty."

He winked at her. "Please indulge me, beautiful." She hesitated and he chided himself for coming on a little too strong with the compliment. "If you don't have anything planned for the rest of the evening I'd like to come and see your greenhouses."

She stared up at him through her lashes. "Tonight?"

He smiled. "Yes, tonight." Sawyer wanted to tell Jessica he wasn't ready for their time together to end.

Jessica nodded. "Okay."

"I'll come over after I help clean up the kitchen." He lowered his head and dropped a kiss on her hair. "Later."

She nodded again and then smiled. "If you have a pair of old boots, then I suggest you wear them, because the floors of the greenhouses are always wet."

"No problem." Sawyer walked Jessica to her car, opened the door and waited for her to get in behind the wheel. He stood in the same spot until the taillights from her vehicle disappeared from view before he went back into the house.

Dusk had begun to settle over the landscape as Sawyer maneuvered into the driveway leading to Jessica's house. He got out of the rental at the same time she rose from a chair on the porch where she had been waiting for him. He smiled when she approached him wearing a pair of orange, mud-splattered boots. She had exchanged her T-shirt for a loose-fitting smock.

Reaching for her free hand, Sawyer laced their fingers together and they headed for the structures set behind a copse of trees. "Let's look at your farm before it gets too dark."

Jessica tapped several buttons on a remote device and a bright light shone from the two glassed-in structures outfitted with solar panels. One greenhouse was the approximate size of a three-car garage and the other large enough for one car. She pushed open the door of the smaller greenhouse.

"I use this one for my flowers," Jessica said as she stood aside and waited for Sawyer to walk in.

A rush of humidity enveloped him at the same time he was greeted by a riot of color and fragrances from potted flowers, ferns and grasses. He recognized roses, tulips, birds of paradise, cacti and different varieties of hanging orchids, but couldn't identify any of the other plants seemingly growing in organized uninhibitedness. Sawyer shook his head in amazement. He glanced over his shoulder at Jessica standing in the doorway. "They're beautiful. Do you grow them from seeds?"

"No. I buy the flats from a nursery. However, I do cultivate the tulips, narcissus and amaryllis from bulbs. Are you ready to see the veggies?"

"Sure." If he was awed by Jessica's flower garden, then he was completely overwhelmed by raised beds with rows of vegetables, and he doubted whether she would ever have to visit a supermarket's produce department. There were massive pots with lime and lemon trees and several others overflowing with strawberries spanning an entire wall. "Damn-m-m," he drawled, drawing out the word to three syllables. "This is definitely a vegetarian's nirvana."

Jessica laughed. "I agree."

"What don't you grow?"

Jessica walked over to stand next to him. "Rice and potatoes."

Sawyer looped his arm around her waist and bit back a smile when she leaned into him. He found the warmth of her body and the faint scent of her perfume intoxicating. There was something about the woman beside him that disturbed Sawyer, but in a good way. Everything about Jessica appealed to him in a way a man related to a woman. She wasn't flirtatious yet she had a way of staring up at him through her lashes that turned him on.

"Do you garden all year?"

"No. Once I harvest this year's yield I don't plant again until next spring." A beeping sound echoed throughout the greenhouse. "We have one minute to get out of here before the sprinklers are activated," Jessica warned. "They're programmed to come on every twelve hours."

They walked out, and thirty seconds later a light spray of water from piping rained down on the produce. Tapping buttons on the remote, Jessica turned off the lights and locked the doors to both structures. A sprinkling of stars dotted the nighttime sky as they made their way around the house.

Sawyer turned to face Jessica, resting his hands on her shoulders.

"Please hang out on the porch with me. I'd like to

talk to you about what you plan to do during your summer break."

Sawyer wanting to talk about her summer vacation confirmed Jessica's suspicions that he and Rachel had discussed her. "Okay." She walked up to the porch and sat down on the love seat. She patted the cushion beside her when he leaned against a column, arms crossed over his chest. "You can sit next to me. I promise not to bite."

Sawyer stood up straight, took several steps and folded his body down to the love seat. Dropping an arm over her shoulders, he pressed a kiss to her neck. "No one warned you that I'm a vampire, and once the sun goes down I crave the blood of beautiful young women."

Jessica's pulse raced as she laughed softly. There was something about Sawyer she was helpless to resist, and *if* she did become involved with Sawyer, then she was certain she could have a mature, noncommittal relationship with her best friend's brother.

"How many women have you bitten?"

He nibbled her earlobe. "You would be the first."

Jessica laughed again. "Wouldn't that make me a vampire, too?"

"Yes, ma'am."

She rested her head on his shoulder. "I'm going to pass on immortality, because I don't like the sight of blood."

Sawyer kissed her hair. "Bummer," he whispered. "Rachel mentioned you weren't going away this summer, so I hope we can hang out together while I'm here."

"You're going to have to let me know when, because I plan to call Taryn in New York and spend some time with her."

"I leave New York to spend the summer here, and you plan to leave The Falls to go to New York."

"I'll probably be gone for about a week." She shifted and stared directly at Sawyer. The porch lights cast long and short shadows over his handsome features. "What made you decide to live in New York?"

Jessica listened intently as Sawyer told her about enlisting in the army within two weeks of graduating high school. He'd stayed long enough to earn a college degree in computer science and then returned to West Virginia to secure a position with a tech company. "I wasn't back three months when I had a very serious falling out with my father, so I packed my bags and took a bus to New York," he continued in the soft, drawling cadence she found so soothing to her ears. "I lived in the Y for several months before I heard that a couple of dudes were looking for a roommate to share an apartment on the Lower East Side. Meanwhile, I applied to New York University to do a graduate degree because if I wanted to teach I'd need a masters."

"You wanted to be a teacher?"

He lifted a shoulder. "I'd thought about it a few times, but everything changed when I bonded with three other students once we became study partners for a course in algorithms and data structure. Together we designed a browser rivaling a major search engine company. We applied for a patent, formed a company known as Enigma4For4, and launched the site. Then we followed up with a dating site, several apps, a medical GPS chip and a number of match-three puzzle video games, each with nearly fifty million average monthly users. And with the dearth of women at the helm of internet startups, we made history when we voted to make Elena CEO in the male-dominated tech world."

Jessica was momentarily speechless. Rachel had mentioned her brother was a software engineer, but not once had she talked about his successes. "Why haven't you been celebrated as a local hero?"

"All of us, with the exception of Elena, have managed to keep a low profile because we want to live normal lives." Sawyer tightened his hold on her shoulders. "With the exception of not having to share a one-room apartment, my life hasn't changed much. I did purchase the loft building across the street from where I work."

"That's it?"

He chuckled under his breath. "That's it. Did you expect me to live in a penthouse, drive a Lamborghini and host parties on a yacht?"

There was no doubt Sawyer was, like his company's name, an enigma. "I don't know what to expect when I read and hear of so many stories about young wealthy entrepreneurs wallowing in wretched excess."

"Not this country boy. Now, tell me why you left the big city for a small town."

Jessica hesitated, choosing her words carefully. She didn't want Sawyer to believe that she had fled Pittsburgh because she wasn't strong enough to stand up to those who had openly bullied her. "I told you I left to go to college but there's more." She told him she'd met Gregory as a freshman and he had proposed marriage midway through their sophomore year. Meanwhile, her fiancé's fraternity brother had taken a liking to her roommate, but Lisa rejected his advances because she was a lesbian, though she was reluctant to come out. "I'd gone home to be with my parents when we flew to

Virginia to bury my brother at the Arlington National Cemetery. He died after his helicopter was shot down in Iraq."

Sawyer gathered her closer. "I'm so sorry, babe," he whispered in her ear.

Jessica paused, struggling not to cry. She didn't like talking about her older brother, whom she'd adored. Sawyer shifted her to sit on his lap, cradling her as if she was a child as she continued, recalling the incident that had changed her and her future. "I returned to campus and when I opened the door to my dorm room I found Rowan raping my roommate. Once I began yelling for him to get off her he had the audacity to tell me she wanted him to sleep with her. I called the campus police to report it and then drove Lisa to the hospital. All hell broke loose when the pig told everyone the sex was consensual, which she denied, and because I witnessed the act I became the campus pariah. Rowan was predicted to become a Heisman Trophy winner, while scouts from NFL teams were falling over themselves to sign him."

"What happened to him?"

"He was never charged because Lisa dropped out and moved back to Cleveland. The man I'd promised to marry accused me of colluding with my roommate to ruin his frat brother's life, so I gave him back his ring. Eventually, I withdrew due to psychological distress when notes threatening my life were slipped under the door of my dorm room. I applied to Howard, and after I was accepted I moved to DC. Rowan went on to play pro ball, but his career ended after two years when he was involved in a car crash that crushed his legs."

Jessica exhaled an audible sigh. "I carried a lot of

resentment until I realized if I didn't forgive Gregory then I would never be able to move on with my life."

A beat passed before Sawyer said, "Good for you. Forgiveness is something that doesn't come easy for some folks." There came another pause. "But I'm sorry you and your roommate had to go through hell because people don't want to believe their heroes are flawed."

Wrapping her arms around Sawyer's neck, Jessica pressed her mouth to the light stubble on his jaw. "If it hadn't happened, then I wouldn't be who I am today. I'd lost one roommate, but rooming with Taryn Robinson I was finally able to enjoy campus life."

"When do you plan to go to New York to see her?"

Jessica closed her eyes. "I can't go until July because I want to complete some research for the district's grant proposal."

"A grant for what?"

She opened her eyes. "We need to update the electronic equipment in the elementary and middle schools."

"What do you need?"

"PCs, laptops, tablets and smartboards."

Sawyer angled his head. "Have you written or submitted the grant application?"

"We've submitted applications the past two years to a privately funded foundation set up to give out grants to educational institutions and although we were in the final three we didn't get it."

"Do you have copies of what you submitted?"

"Yes but—"

"I'd like to look them over," Sawyer said cutting her off. "How much are you asking for?"

"Four hundred fifty thousand. Four hundred for equipment and fifty to pay a trainer."

"That's not much. I can help you out by getting my company to donate what you need."

A gasp slipped through Jessica's parted lips. "I would forever be in your debt if you're able to help us get some of the funding or even a donation of equipment."

"Are you certain you mean forever?"

She glanced away from his smirking expression. "Maybe I should've said for a long time."

"When do you want to start?"

"Call me whenever you have the time. If you come early enough I'll make breakfast. What would you like to eat?"

He pushed to his feet, holding her effortlessly, then set her on her feet. "Surprise me."

Jessica felt a rush of excitement, unable to believe Sawyer had offered to make this donation. "I'll also get the proposals together for you to review. I have to warn you there are more than twenty pages of minutiae along with financial attachments."

"Don't worry about it, babe. I still have one more home improvement project to finish before I'm all yours."

His hands circled her waist and pulled her against his body. Jessica knew Sawyer was going to kiss her, and at that moment she wanted his kiss and more. She wanted to relive the passion she'd almost forgotten. She was breathing heavily, and her lips parted when his head came down as his mouth covered hers in a tender joining that nearly brought her to tears. Anchoring her arms under his shoulders, Jessica pressed closer until they were molded together from chest to knees. Her entire body was flooded with desire and she moaned aloud when he ended the kiss.

Sawyer put a modicum of space between them. "I think I'd better leave now before we do something we're not ready for." He kissed her forehead. "Good night, babe."

Rising on tiptoe, Jessica pressed a light kiss to the corner of Sawyer's mouth. "Good night."

She waited until he drove away and then went into the house. Bootsy met her, standing on his hind legs for her to pick him up. Cradling him to her chest, she kissed his head. "It looks as if your mama is going to get her donation, thanks to Sawyer Middleton. And that means you can't growl or show your teeth at him. Okay, baby?" Bootsy whined softly as he closed his eyes. Jessica smiled. "You are one spoiled puppy."

She carried him into the family room, placed him in his bed in a corner and flicked on the television. Knowing she would get the money was overshadowed by her reaction to being held by and kissing Sawyer. He had become a constant reminder that she was a woman who had denied the strong passions within her for far too long, and she looked forward to spending time with him during her summer break.

A week later Jessica stood on the front porch watching Beatrice get out of her car. The kindergarten teacher had called to say she wanted to tell Jessica something. They exchanged a hug.

"Come in." Jessica was anxious to find out why her friend had come in lieu of having a telephone conversation. She led the way into the sitting room where she and Beatrice sat in facing armchairs. "What's up?"

Beatrice ran a hand over her braided hair. "Jabari got a call from the bank's corporate office last night.

They're moving the mortgage department to Denver and they want him to head it."

Jessica stared at her colleague. "You're moving to Denver?"

"I'll have to if he accepts the position. This will be our third move in ten years. I told him I feel like a military wife, packing up and moving every three or four years."

"Didn't you tell me that when you married Jabari you knew his job required relocating?"

"Yes and…" Beatrice's words trailed off as she shook her head. "I'm trying to be a supportive wife, but it's not easy for Keisha to adjust to a new school every few years. Just when she makes new friends she has to leave. Even if I wasn't leaving I'd hardly get to see you during the day because you'll now be in the middle school building."

"Give me another five years and I'll probably be teaching high school English," Jessica teased.

"I forget you have certification from Pre-K to 12."

"It does make me more marketable."

"Have you ever thought about becoming an administrator?" Beatrice asked.

Jessica put up both hands. "I don't have the temperament to deal with school politics." She didn't want to think of not seeing Beatrice every day, but her friend had hinted earlier in the year that her husband might be promoted and that meant moving from West Virginia but she hadn't believed it would happen so quickly.

Since leaving home for college Jessica had moved three times, and when she walked into the house in Wickham Falls she'd promised herself it would be the last. Living in Wickham Falls suited her personality and lifestyle. She had colleagues whom she also counted as friends, and interacting with the Middletons gave her a sense of family. "We have to have a girls' night over the summer regardless of whether you're staying or leaving."

Beatrice nodded. "That's for sure. By the way, how's your love life?"

"Who are you talking about?"

"Aren't you involved with the Phelan twins' uncle?"

"Why would you think that?" She hadn't confirmed or denied she was involved with Sawyer.

"Only someone who's visually impaired wouldn't be able see the sexual heat coming off you two. Even Abby said something, and you know she's usually as close-mouth as a clam when it comes to gossiping." Beatrice moved her chair, reaching across the space to hold Jessica's hand. "You can tell me to mind my own damn business, but I'm going to say this and be done with it. The man has the same look in his eye Jabari had when we met for the first time."

"And exactly what look was that?"

"*I'm not going to let you get away*. I don't know if I ever told you, but Jabari isn't my first husband. I'd just gotten out of a short-lived marriage with a certified lunatic and I wasn't about to get back on that runaway crazy roller coaster for a second time. Then I met Jabari at a Chicago mayoral fundraiser. It didn't take long for me to realize he is a throwback to another generation when he courted me. Five months after our first date we flew to Vegas and eloped."

"Sawyer did ask me out and I said yes," Jessica admitted.

Beatrice stood up, smiling. Jessica also rose to stand.

"Good for you." Beatrice hugged Jessica. "I'll call you with an update on the move."

"If you don't call, then I'll call you."

Jessica sat on the front porch long after Beatrice had driven away. Dusk had fallen and the intermittent glow of fireflies dotted the shroud of darkness blanketing the countryside. She thought about what Beatrice had said about her and Sawyer.

Had they seen what she did not want to accept or even acknowledge? That she needed more in her life than her students and a pet. That she needed to trust a man enough to have a normal relationship that could result in marriage and children. However, she doubted Sawyer would be that man because he planned to leave Wickham Falls at the end of the summer.

Chapter Eight

Jessica stood at the French doors overlooking the patio. It'd been raining steadily for three days and the gloominess was beginning to affect her mood. Bootsy's growling captured her attention. He'd found his leash and pulled it into the kitchen. "I know. You want to go out."

Grabbing her cell phone off the table, she went into the mudroom, slipped into a pair of boots and pulled a rain slicker over her head. Minutes later she raced behind Bootsy as he headed for his favorite spot. One hundred percent humidity swirled around her face like moist feathers. Oblivious to the rain soaking his coat, Bootsy took his time doing what he normally did within minutes, lingering and sniffing every blade of wet grass and clumps of wildflowers poking their heads up through the rocky earth.

She forced him inside and towel dried the canine,

making certain to wipe the grass and mud from his paws. She'd just dropped the towel into a hamper where she kept the dog's laundry when her cell rang. A slight frown appeared between her eyes. There was no name on the display, and she didn't recognize the number or the 646 area code.

Tapping the phone icon, she said, "Yes?"

"Jessica. It's Sawyer."

Her mouth curved into an unconscious smile. "Hey. How are you?"

"Good," he said. "How are you?"

"Going a little stir-crazy because of the rain," she admitted truthfully.

"Same here. I started power washing the house but had to stop because of the weather. I called because I want to know if you have time for me to go over your grant application with you."

Jessica sat on the stool at the cooking island. "I have nothing but time."

Sawyer's deep laugh came through the earpiece. "Now you sound like me. The weather has me indoors and after watching countless cartoons and playing board games with Dylan and Colin I'm ready for a little adult company."

"That's where we differ. I never get tired of being around children."

Sawyer laughed again. "Spoken like a dedicated teacher. What's a good time for me to come over?"

"I'm free now." She took a quick glance at the microwave's clock. It was 12:10. "Did you eat lunch?"

"No, but I'll stop by Ruthie's and bring something."

"Forget Ruthie's, Sawyer. I have food here."

"I don't want you to cook for me. After all, you're

on vacation. What if I pick you up and we discuss your grant over lunch at the Wolf Den?"

"Okay. I'll bring a copy with me."

"Can you be ready in twenty minutes?"

"Yes." Jessica ended the call and bolted for the staircase.

Sawyer got out of his truck at the same time Jessica walked out the house. He had left the engine running and the wipers were turned to the lowest speed. He pushed the button on a golf umbrella and it opened with a soft swooshing sound. She was dressed for the weather: black jeans, rain boots stamped with a black-and-white-pinstripe pattern, a black poncho and a Pittsburgh Pirates baseball cap.

Curving an arm around her waist, he led her off the porch to the Jeep and helped her up. He closed the umbrella, leaving it on the floor behind the front seats and got in behind the wheel. "I'm certain ducks are really enjoying this weather."

Everything about Jessica appealed to him whether it was her dulcet voice, petite curvy body or composed demeanor. Her intelligence was definitely a plus. In other words—she was the total package. If anyone or anything could get him to change his mind about moving back to Wickham Falls it was Jessica. She was a constant reminder of what had been missing in his life, and that was companionship. It had taken coming back home to make him aware that putting in a sixty-hour work week and dating a revolving door of women was no longer appealing or rewarding.

"Ducks and farmers," Jessica said.

"You're right. If West Virginia wasn't so mountainous I'm certain we would have as many farms as we do mines." Sawyer, shifted into Drive, executed a perfect U-turn and drove along Porterfield Lane until he came to the road leading to the celebrated sports bar. He increased the wiper speed as the rain intensified. He gave Jessica a sidelong glance as she stared through the windshield. "Did you bring the grant proposal?"

Jessica unzipped a large patch pocket in the front of her poncho and removed a letter-size plastic envelope. "It's in here."

Initially he'd thought about asking his partners to donate the monies needed to update the technology lab and then changed his mind. As one fourth of Enigma4For4, seeing to the ongoing success of technology students in the Johnson County school district was his personal responsibility.

"I contacted my financial planner to set up a charity to draw down the monies you need for the grant, and I'll make certain the district will get the monies before the beginning of the new school year."

Jessica stared at his profile. "Can't you get your partners to go in with you?"

Sawyer shook his head. "I'd thought about it, but then changed my mind. It's not as if the company hasn't donated monies to different charities, but Johnson County public schools is personal for me. I doubt if I'd be who I am today if dedicated teachers hadn't encouraged me to work to my full potential. So, the answer to your question is no.

"And I'm willing to donate the money because kids shouldn't have to wait for bureaucrats to wake up and see that our school kids are lagging behind those in other countries when it comes to math, science and technology."

"You're preaching to the choir, Sawyer. And if you really want to effect change then become a teacher."

A mysterious smile lifted the corners of his mouth. "I've thought about it a few times," he said without guile. One of his former grad school professors had asked if Sawyer would fill in for him when he went on sabbatical; however, the timing had been all wrong, because he was committed to his partners at Enigma4For4.

Jessica settled back against the leather seat. An expression of satisfaction showed in her eyes when she stared out the side window. Sawyer offering to underwrite the new equipment went beyond anything she could have thought possible, and with the stroke of a pen he would make it a reality.

"Why is the Wolf Den off the beaten track like a hideout? I wouldn't have known it was hidden in the woods if Rachel hadn't pointed it out to me. Rumors say it was used for moonshiners during Prohibition."

"It *was* a moonshine hangout during that time. I heard that old man Gibson had a still about a mile up the mountain not far from an abandoned mineshaft. The revenuers suspected they were making and selling hooch, yet they were never able to prove it."

"How did they get away with it?"

Sawyer shook his head. "I don't know. There was talk that Earl Gibson paid the government agents to look the other way, while I overheard my mother claim her grandfather was their lookout. He had a place close to the road. He sat on the porch with a pair of binoculars checking out everyone coming and going. It was a known fact that he was an insomniac, so whenever someone drove by in a car and he didn't recognize the license plate he called the Den to give them a heads-up. Very few folks around these parts had a phone during that time and most didn't know Earl paid my great-granddad's phone bill. He gave him ten dollars a week for acting as a sentry and all the moonshine he could drink. After Great-Grandpa Sawyer passed away his son found gallons of hooch he'd stored in his cellar."

"What happened to it?"

"He smashed every bottle or jar he could find. My mother's dad was a Bible-thumping fire-and-brimstone preacher who didn't smoke, drink, cuss or allow anyone to play what he deemed juke-joint music in his house. He believed a woman's place was in the home, they obeyed their husbands without question and children should be seen and not heard. Unfortunately Mom adopted his view about women obeying their husbands to the extreme when she refused to challenge my father on something with which she disagreed."

"She doesn't appear that passive to me," Jessica said.

"That's because she's changed. Mom admitted that she didn't want to raise her children seeing their parents at each other's throats, so most times she held her tongue. Once I left home and Rachel got married and moved out, she began arguing with him. They still don't agree on everything, but thankfully most times there's peace in the house."

"I guess there comes a time in everyone's life when they have to change," Jessica remarked.

"I agree, if it's for the better." Sawyer maneuvered off the paved road onto a dirt one leading up a steep hill before it dropped off to a valley where the Wolf

Den stood in a large clearing. Despite the hour and the weather the parking area was crowded with pickups.

"So this is the famous Wolf Den," Jessica said, as Sawyer backed into a spot between two pickups. "Or should I say *infamous*," she teased.

Sawyer cut off the engine. "That it is. Don't move. I'll help you down."

She unsnapped her seat belt as he got out and came around to the passenger-side door. Jessica wanted to tell Sawyer she could get down unaided but decided to acquiesce to his chivalry.

Anchoring her arms around his neck, she felt the power in his upper body as he lifted her effortlessly, holding her aloft, noses only inches apart.

With wide eyes, she watched as Sawyer lowered his head and touched his mouth to hers, increasing the kiss until her lips slowly parted under the slight pressure. Jessica clung to him as if he were her lifeline. Her heart pounded against her ribs and it wasn't from fear but repressed desire. Everything that made Sawyer who he was seeped into her being: his strength, warmth, smell and the confidence that made him so overtly male.

The kiss ended as quickly as it had begun. Sawyer stared at her under lowered lids as he lowered her until her feet touched the ground. Reaching for her hand, he held it gently as they headed for the entrance to the restaurant. Many of the tables and stools at the bar were occupied. If it hadn't been for the muted TVs on the walls of the dimly lit eating establishment, Jessica would've thought she'd stepped back in time to when men frequented saloons.

Half a dozen booths lined one wall, while a number of tables crowded the space several feet from the bar.

Rachel was right. The air was redolent with the lingering smell of beer—a smell she did not find repugnant. Without warning the café doors to the kitchen opened and the aroma of steak permeated the air.

Jessica noticed the curious stares of the men as Sawyer led her to a booth and sat opposite her. Taking off her baseball cap and poncho, she placed them on the worn leather seat and picked up the plastic-covered menu. "It's looks as if not too many women come here for lunch," she whispered under her breath.

Sawyer rose slightly, reaching into the pocket of his jeans for a handkerchief to wipe off the moisture clinging to his hair. "Women usually come for dinner, but I'm willing to bet none as beautiful as you."

Jessica's cheeks burned with the unexpected compliment. She lowered her eyes. "You're biased because I'm your sister's friend."

"That's where you're wrong, Jessica. My assessment of you has nothing to do with your association with my family. The first time I saw you I thought I'd conjured you up. I couldn't take my eyes off you. I kept thinking how naturally beautiful you are."

Jessica met his luminous sapphire-blue eyes. "You do have a habit of staring."

"I do when there's something worth staring at."

"You're also quite easy on the eyes," she countered in a soft voice. "I like it when you pull your hair in a bun. It's very sexy." Jessica bit down on her lip so she would not laugh aloud when she saw Sawyer's shocked expression. "Did I embarrass you?" she asked when he glanced down at the table.

Sawyer's gaze swung back to her. "No. It's just that I didn't expect you to come out with something like that."

"Why not? You have to know what you look like."

"What I look like is not the issue, Jessica."

"What is?"

"Us," he said after a noticeable pause.

"What about us?" Jessica was relieved when he said "us," because that meant he liked her as much as she liked him.

"I don't like to play head games or send mixed messages when dealing with a woman."

"It's the same with me when dealing with a man," she countered.

"What is it you want?" Sawyer asked.

She paused. "It's what I don't want."

There was a slight lifting of his eyebrows. "What don't you want?"

A beat passed. "Someone I can't trust enough to fall in love with, marry and start a family."

Sawyer leaned forward. "I hope you're not going to blame all men for what one man did to you?"

"I told you I forgave Gregory. It's been years since I've even thought about him until I mentioned his name the other night."

Sawyer reached across the table, held her hands and gave her fingers a gentle squeeze. "So you do want marriage and children?"

She nodded. "I never said I didn't."

"I have to go to New York to sign the necessary documents for the donation." He held up a hand when she opened her mouth. "I know he can always download the papers, but I also need to discuss some investment strategies with him. Why don't you come with me? That way you can see your roommate at the same time."

Her expression brightened. "Are you sure you don't mind me tagging along?"

"Of course not, otherwise I never would've suggested you come with me. Just let me know what you want to do or see and I'll try and make it happen. Are there any Broadway shows you want to go to, or restaurants you'd like to visit?"

She was momentarily speechless in her surprise seeing tenderness in Sawyer's eyes. This was the generous man Rachel had spoken about. He lived in New York year-round, and that meant he could take advantage of everything the exciting cosmopolitan city offered, yet he offered his time and resources to make her trip more than memorable.

"I'll have to think about it."

"Does your friend live in the city?"

"No. She lives on Long Island."

Sawyer crossed his arms over his chest. "If we can complete the grant application before the end of the month, then maybe we can plan to go to New York before or after July Fourth. That way we won't have to deal with holiday traffic."

"I'm going to call Taryn to find out if she's going to be available. We…" Her words trailed off when a middle-aged waitress approached their table.

"Hey, Sawyer. What can I get for you?" Her gaze shifted from Sawyer to Jessica and she squinted at her. "Don't you teach at Johnson Elementary?"

"Yes, I do."

The waitress extended her hand. "Sharleen Weaver."

Jessica took her hand. "Jessica Calhoun."

Sharleen rested her hands at her waist over a bibbed apron. "What can I get for you good folks?" She glanced over her shoulder at a chalkboard near the bar. "Today's beer special is Summer Shandy."

"Do you have lemonade?" Jessica asked the waitress.

"Sure do, honey. Plain or strawberry?"

Jessica met Sawyer's eyes, seeing amusement in the indigo depths. "I'll have plain."

Sharleen gave Sawyer a wide grin. "What about you, baby?"

"Just sparkling water."

"Are you ready to order or do you need more time?" Sharleen questioned.

Jessica order a steak sandwich with a side Caesar salad, while Sawyer opted for grilled chicken and mixed vegetables. It didn't take her long to realize the Wolf Den wasn't a good place to review the grant proposal as they were interrupted each time someone recognized Sawyer. In between bites of food he was relegated to shaking hands and answering queries as to how long he planned to stay. What she found intriguing was his gift for speed reading. Sawyer gave each page a summary glance before going on to the next.

"You're a speed reader."

He glanced up from a page of statistics. "Yeah. Can you get into the district's database to pull out the stats for grades of graduating students beginning with the establishment of the technology labs to date?"

"Yes. Why?"

"You need to determine the preponderance of higher grades in correlation to a lab with updated technology." Lashes that swept the tops of high cheekbones came up when he gave Jessica a direct stare. "You indicate more than half the computers are inoperable and the other half need updated software. I recommended you include an inventory of equipment with the brand of the computers and their serial numbers. If the computers are more than four or five years old, then it's time to replace them, because you need better hardware, which may include a larger hard drive."

Jessica smiled. It appeared as if she and Sawyer were on the same page when it came to tracking graduation stats. "Four hundred thousand may not be enough if we have to replace all the district's computers with new ones," she said under her breath.

"Then you'll have to increase the grant amount to at least twice that much." Sawyer braced his elbow on the table and rested his chin on his fist. "I'll do the research and give you an estimate of what you need."

Reaching across the length of the table, he held her hand, his thumb caressing her knuckles. "You concentrate on the paperwork and I'll take care of the funding."

She rested her free hand over his. "I can't believe this is happening."

Sawyer leaned over the table. "You forget I was once a Wickham Falls student. It's the least I could do to give back to an educational system that didn't fail me."

"Saw Middleton! Sharleen told me you were here."

Sawyer's head popped up when he recognized one of the restaurant's owners. He stood up, pounding the back of the tall, muscular blond man sporting a military haircut. "What's up, Aiden?"

Aiden Gibson held Sawyer at arm's length. "I should ask you the same. How long you staying?"

"I'll be here until Labor Day." He noticed Aiden staring at Jessica. "I don't know if you're familiar with Jessica Calhoun."

"My pleasure, Miss Calhoun. Word around these parts is that you're a helluva teacher."

She flashed a demure smile. "Thank you."

Aiden sat next to Sawyer. "I don't know if you heard that Denise and I are no longer together. After my second tour in Afghanistan she packed her bags, left the kids with my mother and moved back to Houston. A month later she hit with me with divorce papers."

Sawyer was at a loss for words. He didn't want to believe a woman would walk away from her children. "I'm sorry, man."

Aiden forced a smile. "I'm over it. I usually work the lunch and early dinner shifts because I want to be home at night with my girls. My mom's staying with me temporarily to help take care of her grandkids, but she's been hinting about going back to Florida because my stepdad has been complaining that he misses her. So I'm putting out the word—if you know any woman willing to work as a live-in nanny, please let me know. I would prefer my girls homeschooled until it's time for them to go to middle school. By that time they'll need to learn to socialize with other kids their age."

"I'll keep my ears open," Sawyer promised.

Aiden squeezed Sawyer's shoulder. "I better get back to the kitchen. Don't be a stranger." He pushed to his feet, nodding to Jessica. "It's nice meeting you."

Rising slightly, Sawyer removed a money clip from his front pocket and left a bill on the table. He gathered the pages littering the table. "I'm ready to go back to the house whenever you are."

Jessica stood up. "I'm ready."

Chapter Nine

Jessica sat next to Sawyer at the worktable in the sitting room. "I'll print out the template for the grant, and you can use my desktop while I log on to the district's server to pull up the equipment inventory."

Sawyer pointed to the black-and-white and color photographs lining a side table. "You have a good-looking family." He picked up a photo of Jessica's family. "You look different with long hair. How old were you here?"

"I had to be about ten. My brother had just been awarded his lieutenant's bars and we'd gone out to celebrate."

Dropping his arm over her shoulders, he pulled her close and kissed her hair. "I'm sorry you lost your brother."

Jessica melted into his warmth and strength. "I never got to know Elliot very well. He'd just turned twelve when I was born. By the time I started school he was already in college."

Sawyer rose to his feet, pulling her up with him as he steered her over to the love seat. He sat and then gently eased her down to sit beside him. "Tell me about your people."

The sounds in the room were magnified as Jessica listened to rain tapping against the windows and a soft jazz musical number coming from the radio on a shelf crowded with books, potted plants and miniature book-end marble busts of her favorite British and American writers.

"My mother's people were educators," she said. "After the Civil War they left Kentucky, settling in Ohio and Pennsylvania. I have old photos of one of my great-uncles several generations removed in a Civil War uniform. He'd joined an all-Negro Pennsylvania regiment. I keep promising myself to have it restored yet I've never gotten around to it."

"It has to be a remarkable piece of memorabilia."

"It is. Tell me about your family members who were not caught up in aiding and abetting moonshiners."

Sawyer chuckled under his breath as he rubbed Jessica's hair between his fingertips. "The Middletons and Traverses were a colorful bunch. Some of them were on opposing sides during the Civil War even though none owned slaves. Once West Virginia seceded from Virginia they all put on the blue uniform and fought to preserve the Union. There were a few roustabouts and scalawags in the mix whenever miners went on strike. They were notorious for their skill with a rifle and be-came snipers, and picked off the thugs the mine owners hired to protect scabs that were beaten mercilessly by the strikers."

Raising her head, Jessica met his eyes shimmering with amusement. "That's shameful."

He dropped a kiss on the end of her nose. "No, babe. That's survival." He sobered. "Life in Appalachia has never been easy. We still have mining accidents, even though with mountain top removal, mining deaths are lower than underground. But it's the chemicals used to strip the mountains and then dumped into the valleys that are forcing people to relocate. Hydraulic fracturing for natural gas is another problem that's going to bite us in the behind one of these days."

"You say 'us' as if you live here."

"It doesn't matter where I live. I'm still a West Virginian down to the marrow in my bones."

"Have you ever thought about moving back to The Falls?"

"Right now I'm ambivalent."

Shifting slightly, she gave him a long, penetrating stare. "What are you ambivalent about?"

"This is the first time since moving to New York I feel as if I'm actually home. It wasn't that way when I came back after serving in the army. Maybe it had something to do with the hostility between me and my father. Dad and I had a final blowup and he told me to get out and never come back."

Jessica rested her hand over his heart, counting the strong, steady beats under the sweater. "But you did come back."

"I had to. Henry and I are no longer at each other's throats, and for the first time in my life I can say I've bonded with my father."

"Do you think it's because of the heart attack?"

"It has to be, Jessica. I can't think of anything else that would make Henry Middleton this mellow."

Jessica lost track of time as she closed her eyes and tried imagining herself married to Sawyer. Would he be amenable to moving back to West Virginia, or would he insist they live in New York? Would he be willing to wait a couple of years to have children? And there was the question of his company. If he did agree to live in Wickham Falls, would he commute to New York on business or insist they live there?

The questions nagged at her and she chided herself for thinking that far in the future. She wasn't in love with Sawyer and it was obvious he wasn't in love with her, so why was she indulging in flights of fancy when they barely knew each other? She eased out of his embrace. "I'm going to download the stats you need onto a thumb drive and unlock the restrictions limiting an unauthorized user."

"I'll need your email address so I can send you my drafts for your approval."

"Will do," Jessica confirmed as she pushed to her feet. His holding her made her feel protected—something that had been missing for years.

Sawyer walked over to the wall calendar and studied the entries as he waited for Jessica to download the information he needed to analyze the student data for the donation. A slight smile parted his lips when he realized she'd entered a task for every day of the week.

"Do you really follow this schedule?"

Jessica scrolled through pages until she found what she needed to highlight. "Yes."

He peered closer. "You go to the movies every Friday night?"

Swiveling on her chair, Jessica met his eyes. "I don't go *out* to the movies. I have movie night at home complete with popcorn and occasionally relapse and have a couple of Twizzlers."

"No chicken wings?" he teased.

"Whenever Carly, Beatrice, Abby and I hold our monthly girls' night out here on Fridays we go all out with the proverbial movie junk food. We'll have everything from wings, nachos, Twizzlers and popcorn. One time we were very, very bad when Abby brought a box of Godiva truffles. We then agreed to eat healthy for the next two weeks."

Sawyer angled his head as he studied the woman he likened to an onion, someone with whom he had to patiently wait while she revealed another layer of her personality.

"Did you?"

Jessica turned back to the computer monitor. "Yes. It's easy for me because I cook for myself, but the others have families and they occasionally go out to eat during the week."

"If we have movie night here what are we going to eat?"

"Would you be opposed to wine, cheese and fruit?"

Moving closer, Sawyer rested his hands on Jessica's shoulders. "Of course not. Even though I don't drink a lot of beer or hard liquor I am partial to wine." He had developed an affinity for it after spending a two-week leave in France's Loire Valley. He'd slept in historic chateaux, toured vineyards and sampled different varieties. "If you provide the food then I'll bring the wine. How about next Friday night? This Friday I'd like to take you to a restaurant in Charleston. If I make reservations for seven, then we'll have to leave here around six."

She glanced up at him over her shoulder. "Okay."

He dropped his hands. "Would you mind if I look around your place while I wait for you to print out what I need?"

"Not at all. But don't be surprised if Bootsy follows you. My baby is very protective of his home."

Sawyer shook his head when he heard Jessica refer to Bootsy as her baby and the dog's ears perked up. He clapped his hands. "Let's go, Bootsy." The puppy sprang to his feet and trotted after Sawyer, who walked out of the room and strolled through the open living and dining rooms to the staircase. Jessica had used the wall along the staircase as an art gallery. Black-framed black-and-white photographs of world capitals stood out in stark contrast against the pale wall.

His footsteps were muffled on the black-and-white geometric-patterned runner spanning the length of the hallway. The doors to the bedrooms stood open and allowed him a view of the furnishings. He stopped at the entrance to what he knew was Jessica's bedroom. It was decorated in white and varying shades of blue on the bed dressing, and chair cushions contrasted with the white furniture. Sawyer felt as if he were back in a Parisian chateau with pieces reminiscent of eighteenth-century France.

He scooped up Bootsy under his arm like a football and descended the staircase. Jessica held a decorative shopping bag in one hand. "Your home is beautiful."

"Thank you." She pointed to Bootsy. "You're going

to spoil him if you carry him around," she accused in a soft tone.

Sawyer dropped a kiss on the top of the puppy's head and set him on his feet. "You don't carry him around?"

She shook her head. "And I won't let him on the bed with me because he'll want to sleep with me every night."

"It probably wouldn't take long to spoil him."

Jessica handed him the bag. "Everything you'll need is in there. I put the thumb drive in a separate envelope. I've also included my email address."

Moving closer, Sawyer reached for her hand, giving her fingers a gentle squeeze. "I'll try and see how quickly I can get this done for you."

Rising on tiptoe, Jessica pressed a kiss to the corner of his mouth. "I'll never be able to thank you enough for volunteering to help us."

He inhaled the subtle scent of her perfume wafting to his nostrils. "Don't forget Wickham Falls is also my home, so it's the least I can do to give back."

Jessica looped her arm through his as he headed for the door. "I'm certain you'll remind me whenever I forget."

Sawyer slipped into his boots and, ducking his head, raced to the Jeep. He started the engine, shifted into gear and backed out of the driveway. He took his time driving back to his parents' house. The time he had spent with Jessica was enlightening because she was able to open up about her past, while he had been forthcoming about his relationship with his father.

Sawyer smiled. He didn't know what to expect when he had asked Jessica to come with him to New York, and he was pleasantly surprised when she accepted.

He pulled into the driveway behind Henry's faded red pickup. Leaving his boots on the mat on the porch, he walked into the house, encountering complete silence. Sawyer knew his mother was home because she had parked her car on the other side of the house with Rachel's. He crept on sock-covered feet up the staircase to the second floor. All of the doors to the bedrooms were closed. Retracing his steps he entered the family room and saw his father sleeping in the recliner with an open magazine resting on his chest. Henry's eyes opened as Sawyer attempted to back out of the room.

"Come in, son, and sit awhile."

"I don't want to disturb you. Go back to sleep."

Henry grunted. "That's all I've done since getting out of the hospital." He shifted on the chair. "This is the last night I'm sleeping down here."

"Are you sure you're ready to tackle the stairs again?" Sawyer asked.

"I did them twice already today and I wasn't even winded. My doctor says he's going to give me medical clearance next week. After that I'll have to check in with him every three months, then six."

It was apparent his father had cooperated with his doctor and therapist, and it had resulted in a quick recovery. "Where's everyone?"

"Mara, Rachel and the boys are upstairs napping. I think it's all this confounded rain we're having that's making everyone drowsy."

"You're right about that." Sawyer folded his body down to the love seat. "I want to power wash the siding, yet that's not going to happen until the weather clears."

Thick blue veins stood out in stark relief on Henry's gnarled hands as he gripped the armrests. "I want to thank you for all the work you've done around here. I'd planned to fix the shutters and porch but I just couldn't find the energy to start."

"That's because of your heart, Dad."

"I remember a time when I was strong as a bull and I could lift your mama with one hand."

"What's the expression, Dad? Once a man, twice a child."

"Hell, yeah. We're born bald with no teeth and pissing ourselves, and when we get old we lose our hair and teeth and go back to pissing ourselves. You're lucky, because you've got some years before that happens."

"I'm definitely not looking forward to that," Sawyer said jokingly.

Henry's expression stilled, growing serious. "Do you like living in New York?"

"I do. Why do you ask?"

Henry rubbed a hand over his stubbly jaw. "I've watched you since you've been back and you look very comfortable tinkering around the house."

"I like working with my hands."

"What you should be doing is working on your own house. At your age I was married and a father." The older man squinted at Sawyer under lowered eyebrows. "Do you have a special lady you're thinking about settling down with?"

"No, Dad."

"Why not?"

Sawyer wondered how many more times he would have to answer the same question. Crossing his arms over his chest, he blew out a breath. "Because I haven't found that special lady I'd want to spend the rest of my

life with. And when I meet her, then I'll be more than
willing to change my marital status."

"Are you at least looking, Sawyer?"

"Not actively."

"Do you take ladies out?"

"Yes, Dad. I take ladies out on dates." Sawyer wanted
to ask his father what was up with the interrogation.
First it was Rachel and now Henry questioning his love
life. Only his mother respected his privacy. Not once
had she asked him when she could look forward to gain-
ing a daughter-in-law.

His answer seemed to satisfy Henry when he smiled.
"Good. I was beginning to think you were one of those
men who prefer other men."

Sawyer chuckled. "I'm not gay. And I had no idea
you were homophobic."

"I'm not," Henry replied. "When you live on a ship
with dozens of men for months at a time, things can
happen between a few of them. Your old man is a lot
more tolerant than you probably believe." He paused,
seemingly deep in thought. "I wanted to talk to you
about something and this is as good a time as any with
everyone upstairs."

Stretching out his legs and crossing his feet at the
ankles, Sawyer wasn't as calm as he appeared. Things
between him and his father had gone well and he did
not want anything to reverse that. A heavy silence enveloped the room as he waited in dread. "What do want
to talk about?"

Henry closed his eyes. "Us. You. Me." When he
opened his eyes they were filled with unshed tears. "I
want to apologize about how I treated you when you
were growing up. The only thing I can think of is that

you were a constant reminder of what I wanted to be. I was never a good student, yet you made straight As without even trying. I envied you when you were able to enlist in the army like that," he said, snapping his fingers, "while I couldn't join the navy because I couldn't hear well."

Sawyer could not believe what he was hearing. How could a father be jealous of his own son? If anything, he should have been proud of his accomplishments.

Tenting his fingers, he stared directly at his father. "Did you ever stop and think that maybe the hand you were dealt was best for you? You married an incredible woman who gave you a son and a daughter. She kept your house clean and took care of your children while you were out at sea. As a responsible husband you didn't run around with women, gamble or throw away your pay on alcohol and drugs. You have to give yourself props, Dad, for being a good provider. You kept a roof over our heads, and put food on the table and clothes on our backs. And unlike some fathers you didn't have to put up your house to bail your kids out of jail because we killed someone or were involved in drugs or drunk driving."

Henry wagged his head. "All that means nothing when I think of how I treated you."

"If you want absolution, then I forgive you. I remember you saying 'Middleton men don't entertain pity.'" The instant the word "forgive" slipped off his tongue he thought about Jessica forgiving her fiancé for not standing by her. It felt good to say it, but Sawyer knew it would take time for him let go of some of the resentment he had harbored for most of his life.

"I don't remember saying that."

"Well, I do," Sawyer insisted. "Now, if you don't mind, I'd like to bury this topic and talk about something else."

"Like what?"

"Have you thought about how you'd like to celebrate your thirty-fifth wedding anniversary?"

Henry pressed a button on the side of the recliner, raising the footrest and wiggling his toes in a pair of socks with nonskid bottoms. "I'd love to take your mother away. We never had a real honeymoon."

"Where would you like to go?"

"Your mama always talks about spending time in the tropics."

"That sounds like the Caribbean or the South Pacific. How does Tahiti, Fiji or even Bora Bora sound to you?"

"Who's going to Bora Bora?" Rachel asked, as she walked in and flopped down on the love seat next to Sawyer.

"Mom and Dad for their anniversary."

Rachel was barely able to control her gasp of surprise. "You're kidding, aren't you?" She turned her attention to Henry. "Please tell me Sawyer's kidding, Daddy."

Henry glared at Rachel. "He's not kidding. I'd love to take your mama to Bora Bora if it didn't strain our budget."

"What if Rachel and I go in together and pay for your trip as a gift?" Sawyer asked, sharing a look with his sister.

"No, no and no," Henry protested. "I'm not going to take money from my kids."

"You're not taking our money, Daddy," Rachel countered. "It's a gift."

"It's still not my money."

Sawyer rolled his eyes upward. It was apparent Henry hadn't changed that much. He didn't know whether it was false pride or that he didn't want to be indebted to his children that made him obstinate. "You're not the only one in your marriage. Don't you think Mom deserves a couple of weeks of R & R, and the only thing she has to concern herself with is what swimsuit to put on the next day?"

"And if you don't want to go to Bora Bora then you and Mom can come to Hawaii with me and the boys." Rachel had picked up on Sawyer's cue.

Sawyer met Henry's eyes. Since her taco night announcement, Rachel hadn't mentioned taking her sons to Hawaii. "You're going?" he questioned.

"Yes. I just got an email from the head of personnel. They've approved my four-week vacation request."

"When are you leaving?" Henry asked her.

"I've made reservations for the end of the week. Daddy, I checked with your cardiologist and he says he doesn't have to see you again until October, which means you are medically cleared to travel. And there's more than enough room in Mason's house for you and Mom to stay with us."

Henry shook his head. "If Mara and I decide to go, we'll stay in a hotel. We can come and see you and the grandkids if we're not too busy celebrating our anniversary."

"There you go, Dad," drawled Sawyer.

They were still discussing the details for the trip when Mara joined them twenty minutes later. Overwhelmed with the disclosure she would celebrate her upcoming wedding anniversary at a resort on Oahu, she couldn't hold back tears. When Sawyer asked if his parents planned to spend a month on the island, they said they were flexible about returning to the mainland. He told them he would email his travel agent and hopefully get them on the same flight as Rachel and their grandsons.

Then Henry announced he was experiencing cabin fever and suggested everyone go to Ruthie's for dinner.

"I'm going to take a rain check," Sawyer announced as he stood up.

"No, you *didn't* mention rain," Mara said accusingly.

Hands held high in a gesture of surrender, he backpedaled out of the room. "My bad."

He climbed the staircase to the attic, stripped off his sweater and jeans, and lay across the bed. Resting his head on folded arms, he stared up at the ceiling. The day had become one of awakening experiences, leaving him slightly disconcerted.

His father's admission that he had been jealous of his son was something he still wasn't able to wrap his head around. He grew up believing Henry was a throwback to another generation when parents ruled their children with an iron fist—not that he'd resented the accomplishments of his firstborn.

Sawyer lost track of time as he lay listening to the calming sound of rain on the roof; his eyelids fluttered as he struggled to stay awake. He managed to get up and slip under a sheet and quilt before falling asleep. He woke hours later, disoriented yet loath to leave the bed. Night had fallen. He picked up the travel clock on the bedside table. It was after nine when he finally got out of bed and took a shower.

Aware that he wasn't going back to sleep, he slipped

into a pair of cutoffs and a T-shirt and made his way down the staircase to the kitchen. Fortified with a steaming cup of coffee, Sawyer retreated to the family room to watch television.

He picked up the television remote and began channel surfing, stopping at one featuring a *Person of Interest* marathon. He never was much of a television junkie; he preferred documentaries to endless sitcoms and talk shows.

"This is what I'm talking about," he said under his breath.

The premise of the series featured a reclusive billionaire software genius who created a computer to analyze surveillance data patterns for the US government to identify impending acts of terrorism. Within minutes Sawyer found himself completely engrossed in the clever drama. He was still staring at the images on the flat screen when he heard Rachel leave for her shift.

Watching television served to take his mind off a woman who'd unknowingly ensnared him in a web of longing from which he did not want to escape. Not only did Jessica look different from many of the women he'd dated over the years, she was very different because she appealed to everything he wanted in and needed from a woman.

I'm willing to bet some pretty young country girl is going to catch your eye and you'll stop all that talk about being a cool bachelor. He wanted to tell Elena she hadn't been that far off. Jessica Calhoun *was* that pretty young country girl.

Chapter Ten

Three days later a text ringtone shattered Jessica's concentration. She had spent the past ninety minutes going over the grant application. She glanced at the sender's name, and picked up the cell phone.

Sawyer: Good morning, gorgeous.

Jessica: Good morning, sweet prince.

Sawyer: I thought it was good night, sweet prince.

Jessica: So, you're familiar with the Bard?

Sawyer: I happen to love Shakespeare.

Jessica: Don't you ever sleep?

Sawyer: Why?

Jessica: Your emails are time stamped after midnight leading me to believe you're really a vampire.

Sawyer: No such luck. If I were I would bite your neck and we'd live forever.

Jessica: I just finished reading the grant narrative and I can't believe how you've improved on our language.

Sawyer: It's called techie talk.

The prior years' grant proposals had each taken five committee members more than a month to complete. Sawyer had done the job in three days. His budget included a breakdown for new computers and printers for technology labs for the three campuses, personal iPads for high school seniors and smartboards for elementary classrooms. He had also included a line in the budget for a full-time technology instructor and a part-time IT person.

Sawyer: Now that the grant's completed are you ready to head to the Big Apple?

Jessica: When do we leave?

Sawyer: Sunday. My folks, Rachel and the boys are leaving for Hawaii tomorrow morning so there's nothing keeping me here for the next month.

Jessica: How long do you expect us to stay?

Sawyer: As long as you want. We'll drive up and stay at my place. That way you can bring Bootsy.

Now she knew why he'd worked overtime to revise the application. Sawyer planned to combine their trip to New York with business *and* pleasure, and Jessica mentally outlined what she had to do before closing up the house. She had to go to the post office to stop mail delivery and alert her neighbor that she would be away for a while.

Jessica: Thank you!

Sawyer: Talk to you later, doll face.

Jessica: Later, gorgeous.

She sent Logan an email, attaching the proposal and a brief message that she was going to be away and would reconnect with him when he returned to the States. She reinserted the thumb drive into the port and programmed the printer to print enough copies for each committee member.

It had taken Jessica nearly an hour to decide what to wear on her date with Sawyer. One dress appeared a little too risqué and another too drab. She finally chose a navy blue silk-shantung pantsuit with a white silk halter blouse and the heels she'd worn to the retirement dinner. She'd washed her chemically straightened hair, let it air dry and then styled the short strands in a mass of curls with a curling iron. Pearl studs, a matching single strand around her neck and a light cover of makeup completed her beauty regimen just before the doorbell rang.

Bootsy raced into the bedroom, barking incessantly as she gathered her evening purse and keys. "It's all right, baby boy. That's Sawyer." She patted his head. "And remember what I told you about growling and showing your teeth."

She carefully made her way down the staircase in the stilettos to the front door, as Bootsy watched her from the top of the landing. She opened the door to find Sawyer in a pair of dark tailored trousers he had paired with a white shirt and a silk tie that matched his eyes. A pair of black leather slip-ons had replaced his work boots and running shoes. A slow smile parted her lips when she noticed he'd cut his hair, the thick dark strands creating natural waves over the crown of his head.

"I'm ready."

Sawyer stared like a deer caught in the headlights. "You look incredible."

Jessica smiled up at him through her lashes. "Thank you."

Sawyer took the keys from her hand. Stepping out onto the porch, Jessica watched as he closed and locked the door, and then handed her back the keys. He cupped her elbow as he led her off the porch to the Jeep. Bending slightly, Sawyer scooped her up, her arms going around his neck, and deposited her on the passenger seat.

He kissed the tip of her nose. "I figured you'd need assistance because of your shoes," he teased.

"Thank you." Jessica wanted to tell him climbing up into the SUV would have been a lot more challenging if she had worn a pencil skirt. She noticed he'd left his suit jacket on a hanger behind the driver's seat. She buckled her seat belt at the same time Sawyer climbed behind the wheel and secured his. He had tuned the radio to a station featuring love songs.

"I've made reservations for us to eat at a boutique hotel near downtown Charleston," he said once he turned off on the road leading to the interstate. He gave her a quick glance when she touched the tapered strands on the nape of his neck.

"I like your hair."

Sawyer smiled. "I took the boys to the barber for a haircut before their trip and decided it was time I do the same."

Jessica dropped her hand. "When was the last time you cut it?"

"It was almost two years. A few times I thought about cutting it something came up and it was always the next time."

"Were you that busy?"

"I work an average of fifty to sixty hours a week. There are times when I'm coding I forget to eat. Some of our employees sleep over, because they claim going home shatters their concentration."

Jessica gave him an incredulous look. "You allow employees to sleep at the office?"

"Yes." Sawyer told her that he and his partners had purchased a four-story walk-up and converted the first floor to offices for the partners and sixteen employees, and the second into three studio-type apartments for those who elected to work late and an office health club.

"Darius lives on the third floor and Elena and her husband, Thom, occupy the fourth. If I hadn't bought my loft the year before I would've used the second floor.

Six months ago we hired a chef to prepare meals so we don't have to leave the premises. We also use the roof whenever we hold outdoor celebrations."

"So, it's not all work and no play?"

Sawyer signaled before moving over to a faster lane. "This summer is the first time we decided to go on hiatus since starting up the company."

"Why?"

"We're taking the time off to give everyone a much-needed break and to delay taking the company public."

"What do you want, Sawyer?"

"I prefer we stay private. Right now, only Thom wants to go public. We'll vote again when we go back after Labor Day—if it's still three to one, then the topic is off the table for another two years."

"I went online to look up your company and there was less than a page of information. You guys are truly an enigma."

"That's the way we want it—for now."

Their conversation segued from work to football, and despite his hectic work schedule Sawyer admitted to being a sports junkie. Jessica amazed him with her knowledge of professional Pennsylvania teams and by the time Sawyer maneuvered into the area for valet parking he'd accused her of being a trivia junkie. The Lodge hotel was located in a suburb several miles outside the capital.

Sawyer rested a hand at the small of Jessica's back as they followed the hostess to their table. The boutique hotel was reminiscent of a hunting lodge with mahogany-paneled walls, coffered ceilings and stuffed animal heads adorning the walls in the lobby.

"How long has this place been here?" Jessica asked

Sawyer when he sat opposite her. Subtle lighting from sconces and oil-filled candles on each table set the mood for intimate dining.

"More than a century," he answered. "It was where the owner of a local mine entertained his friends. He left the state after he was forced to close the mine because of unsafe working conditions. It went through a series of owners until someone turned it into a hotel to accommodate the overflow of tourists who come down for local fairs and Revolutionary and Civil War reenactments."

Jessica opened the menu binder and studied the selections. Although she had spent the last four years of her life as a West Virginian, she had seen little of the Mountain State beyond the capital region. "Will you be available to become my personal guide when I go sightseeing around the state this summer?"

Sawyer's head popped up. "Of course. I'd promised Colin and Dylan that I'd take them fishing, hiking and whitewater rafting, but that's not going to happen now that they're vacationing in Hawaii."

"Have you heard from them?"

"I got a text from Rachel earlier this morning that everyone's still a little jet-lagged. Once she told Dylan and Colin they were going to Hawaii they couldn't wait to tell me I didn't have to take them fishing or hiking because they were going to learn to surf."

"It's going to take them a few days before their circadian rhythms adjust to the time zone," she said after a comfortable silence. "And you can't blame them for being excited about hanging out on the beach." A waiter approached their table to take their beverage order. Jessica deferred to Sawyer when he ordered a sparkling rosé to accompany their entrées.

She ordered pecan-crusted trout, rice pilaf and broccoli, while Sawyer selected a grilled pork chop with an apple-bourbon glaze, fingerling potatoes and a fennel-apple slaw. Over the next hour, and in-between bites of food and sips of wine, Jessica revealed she had grown up in an upper-middle-class Pittsburgh suburb. Her college-professor parents had enrolled her in a private, all-girl school, while her brother attended a nearby military school for boys.

Sawyer countered, saying his upbringing was not as privileged. He'd attended public schools and knew he wanted a career in technology after his mother gave him a computer for his thirteenth birthday. Two weeks following his high school graduation, he enlisted in the army and earned a college degree with a major in computer science. Once he was honorably discharged he'd returned to Wickham Falls, but after a volatile verbal confrontation with Henry he'd moved to New York, enrolled in grad school and eventually become a partner in an internet startup.

"You've done well, Sawyer."

He nodded. "And you haven't?"

"I've realized my goal to teach, but did you ever think you would own a tech company?"

Leaning back in his chair, he stared at her for a long moment, and Jessica wondered what was going on behind the indigo-blue orbs.

"No. If the situation had been different and I hadn't had that dustup with my father I would've settled down in The Falls, hired myself out as an internet technician, married some local girl and become a daddy with a couple of kids by now." He paused. "I don't regret leaving because it changed my life." A slight smile lifted the corners of his mouth. "And now I'm back."

But only for the summer, Jessica mused. She knew whatever she would share with Sawyer would end once he returned to New York, leaving her with memories of a man she liked more than any she had met in a very long time.

Sawyer settled the check and during the return drive to Wickham Falls he and Jessica engaged in a karaoke challenge when he tuned the satellite radio to a station featuring classic pop songs spanning several decades. By the time he parked in front of Jessica's house they'd agreed it was a draw.

He got out, came around and helped her down. "I really enjoyed tonight."

Jessica wrapped an arm around his waist as they climbed the porch steps. "So did I."

Sawyer took the keys from her hand and unlocked the door. "We have to do it again when we get to New York."

"I'm really looking forward to seeing Taryn. I'm going to call her tomorrow to let her know I'm coming up."

Cradling her head between his palms, he brushed light kisses over her mouth until her lips parted and he deepened the kiss. Sawyer knew if he continued to kiss Jessica he would want more—and the more was stripping her naked and making love to her. It took herculean strength for him to pull away.

"Good night, babe. I'll call you tomorrow to let you know what time I'll pick you up Sunday."

Turning on his heel, he returned to the Jeep and

backed out of the driveway after Jessica went into the house and closed the door. Sawyer did not have to go to a clairvoyant for them to tell him that he was falling in love with Jessica Calhoun. Being with her filled him with the peace that had eluded him most of his life. When growing up in The Falls he had fantasized about leaving because he felt it was too small, that there was another world outside his hometown that called out to him. He'd joined the military to earn a college degree and to see the world, but despite visiting other countries his sense of restlessness continued. He'd found some respite in New York only because he had totally immersed himself in his work. And, now that he had come back to his hometown, not once had he felt the agitation that wouldn't allow him to stop looking for something that did not exist.

He had come home to reconnect with his family, make peace with his father, give back to the school system that had given him so much and find a pretty country girl who unknowingly had him seriously considering giving up his so-called cool bachelor lifestyle.

"Are you sure you want to drive the first lap?" Sawyer asked Jessica.

She adjusted the driver's seat to accommodate her legs. "Yes." She'd volunteered to drive to Hagerstown, and then Sawyer would take over and drive to New York City. "Why don't you try and get some sleep and I'll wake you once we get to Maryland." Jessica peered up at the rearview mirror. Bootsy settled down in his crate as she maneuvered out of the driveway.

Sawyer reclined his seat and closed his eyes. "If you

get tired, then wake me up." He shifted into a more comfortable position.

She gave him a quick glance, her breath momentarily catching in her chest. Arms folded over his chest, he hadn't opened his eyes. The length of dark lashes resting on tanned high cheekbones and the stubble on his lean jaw made him a visual feast. And it wasn't the first time Jessica had asked herself as to what it was about Sawyer that elicited a longing she had never known.

"Have you ever been to Hawaii?" Sawyer questioned.

"No."

"Would you like to go?"

"Are you offering to take me?" she teased.

Sawyer opened his eyes and raised the seat back. "Yes."

"I'm sorry, but that's not going to happen until I'm fifty-five."

"Why fifty-five?"

"That's when I plan to retire and travel around the world."

"That shouldn't preclude you taking a couple of weeks off and going there before you retire."

"If I'm going to someplace exotic, then I'm going to need more than a couple of weeks. That can only happen if I go during my summer break. And I really don't want to jostle for space during the height of the tourist season."

Sawyer wanted to tell Jessica that he could make it happen for her before she turned fifty-five. "What if you're married or have children? Do you still plan to retire at fifty-five?"

"Being married or becoming a mother may modify my travel plans, but I still intend to retire at fifty-five.

I promised myself I would teach for thirty years and not one year longer."

"You prefer touring Europe during the off-season?"

Jessica nodded. "My fervent wish is to go to Paris in the winter and celebrate Carnivale in Venice. My parents took me to France as a high school graduation gift and all I remember are long lines of tourists waiting to get into churches, restaurants and museums." She paused. "Have you ever been there?"

"Yes. I'd walk the streets for hours or sit at outdoor cafés drinking coffee."

"Did you have a problem communicating with the locals?" she asked.

"My high school French came in handy, but then most Europeans understand and speak English in addition to their own native tongue. Are you all right?" he asked when Jessica rolled her head from side to side.

"My shoulders are a little stiff. I must have slept wrong."

Sawyer caressed the nape of Jessica's neck before moving lower to her shoulders. "Your muscles are really tight. Pull over and I'll drive."

Jessica moaned softly. "Please don't stop. Oo-oo, that feels wonderful."

His fingers stilled with her exhalation of breath, and then started up again. The silken feel of her skin under his fingers conjured up images of his making love to her.

From the moment he first set eyes on his sister's friend, Sawyer had told himself Jessica was verboten. That no matter how much she turned him on, he promised himself he would not touch her, because he would be in The Falls for the summer and becoming that involved with her would complicate his having to leave. Now, he wasn't as confident he would be able to keep that promise.

"Once we get to my place you'll have a chance to unwind. Do you want to eat out or do you want me to order in?"

"If we eat in, then I want pizza."

A beat passed. "Why pizza?"

"I love New York pizza."

"It is the best," Sawyer said in agreement. "The pizza shops in my neighborhood are good, but they can't compare to a joint in Little Italy famous for their oven-baked thin crust. I'll be certain to take you there before we leave. Tonight we'll eat in. Talking about food reminds me that I have to order groceries *and* dinner." Opening the glove box, he retrieved his cell phone.

Jessica signaled before moving into a faster lane. "I thought you had a chef."

"We only utilize the services of a chef for the office. I deal with a market that delivers around the clock. That's the upside of living in a city that never sleeps." He contacted a local gourmet market to order food to restock the refrigerator and freezer, and then selected a one-hour window for a delivery between seven and eight that evening.

"What do you have planned for Monday?" Jessica asked.

"I'm meeting with my financial planner. I'm not certain how long I'll be tied up with him, so if you want to meet your girlfriend then I'll arrange for a car service to take you to Long Island."

"I'm not going to see her. Her widowed grandmother sold her house, and Taryn and her mother have to pack up the contents because the new owners want to move in next week. So I invited her to come to Wickham Falls later next month."

"I suppose this means I'll have to change our plans."

"What had you planned?" Jessica asked.

Sawyer dropped his hand. "I did check the baseball schedules and the Pirates are playing the Mets next week. If I go online I'll probably be able to get tickets for us. By the way, it's a night game."

Jessica flashed a wide grin. "That sounds like a plan. I'm just sorry I didn't bring any of my Pirates paraphernalia."

"Don't sweat it, sweetheart. You'll do well not to advertise you're a Pirates fan at Citi Field. There's a bit of a rivalry between the two teams."

"Like the Yankees and the Boston Red Sox? Or the Islanders and the Flyers."

"There you go."

"What's up with New York teams not playing well with others?" she joked.

"Now it's on like Donkey Kong," Sawyer whispered under his breath. "You can't come to New York and talk smack about their teams, because folks will bring holy hell down on you."

Jessica made a sucking sound with her tongue and teeth. "I'm not worried because I expect you to have my back."

He chuckled under his breath. "You're right. I do have your back."

Sawyer wanted to tell Jessica he would always protect her in any given situation. And he looked forward to attending a sporting event with her. Whether it was baseball, basketball or a football game it was a rare occasion when he took time out of his workday to join the loyal fans rooting for their home teams. He, Thom and Darius had season tickets to New York Giants home games.

Sawyer and Jessica talked about everything from books to movies during the drive to Maryland, and when they stopped in Hagerstown they took turns to stretch their legs. Sawyer released Bootsy from the crate and walked the dog after giving him water and a doggie treat. Forty minutes later they were back on the road.

Sawyer double-parked across the street from the offices of Enigma4For4. Although he lived across the street from his partners, they rarely socialized outside the office, because after spending so many hours working together they'd come to respect one another's privacy. The exception was sporting events.

"I'm going to take you and Bootsy upstairs before I park the car."

"Where are you going?" Jessica asked, staring through the windshield. Vehicles were tightly lined up in front of brownstones, townhouses and tenement buildings on both sides of the tree-lined street.

"There's an indoor garage around the corner that's open 24/7." He assisted Jessica out of the sport utility vehicle, then came around to the cargo area to remove her wheeled Pullman and the canvas bag with Bootsy's food and supplies as the puppy barked excitedly, struggling to get out of the crate.

"Patience, buddy," Sawyer crooned. "I'll let you out as soon as we're upstairs." He looped the handles of the canvas bag over the handles of the Pullman to make it easier for Jessica to manage both bags.

The doorman manning the lobby of the building

opened the door, flashing a wide grin. "Good evening, Mr. Middleton. Glad to see you back."

Sawyer nodded to the man from the security company responsible for protecting the building's tenants. "Thank you. It's good to be back." He glanced at his watch. It was 5:40. "I'm expecting a grocery delivery between seven and eight."

"No problem, Mr. Middleton. I'll ring you when they arrive."

He balanced the crate against his chest as he led the way to the elevator and reached into the pocket of his shirt for a key card. The doors to the elevator opened, and he followed Jessica inside and inserted the key card in a slot for the third floor.

She gave him a puzzled look as the car rose slowly to the designated floor. "I was of the belief that apartment buildings, not lofts, have doormen."

"There's an art gallery on the first floor and the owners wouldn't move in unless the building was secure." He didn't tell her that the gallery owners refused to sign a lease until he'd installed closed-circuit cameras throughout the building and contracted with the security company to safeguard their multimillion-dollar inventory.

"It's nice knowing you can go away and no one will break into your place."

He nodded. The doors opened at the third floor and Sawyer stepped out into the expansive entryway to the loft. He set down the crate and opened the door. Bootsy took a few tentative steps before coming out to explore his new surroundings.

He rested a hand at the small of Jessica's back. "Make yourself at home. I'll be back in few minutes."

With wide eyes, Jessica stared at the spectacular sight before her eyes. Cherrywood flooring, exposed brick walls and floor-to-ceilings windows beckoned her to come and stay forever. When Sawyer had mentioned his apartment was larger than a studio she never could have imagined the size and scope of the place he now called home.

Bootsy's whining galvanized her into action, so she opened the canvas bag and assembled the frame to secure the wee-wee pads. She did not want her pet to soil the exquisite wood flooring.

Jessica left her luggage by the door as she walked into an expansive open space with a living room, dining room and kitchen. There was another area opposite the dining room with state-of-the-art audio components on a mahogany console and a chocolate-brown leather seating grouping. Her gaze shifted to large-screen television affixed to a wall over a fireplace. She peered into a recessed space with floor-to-ceiling windows as the backdrop for a library/home office.

The granite-topped cabinetry paneled in sycamore wood afforded the kitchen a sleek but warm feeling. Most of the appliances, including the dishwasher, double refrigerator and freezer were covered with the same light wood, which gave the space a clean aesthetic appearance. The granite-covered breakfast bar with four leather-covered stools provided seating in addition to the rectangular mahogany table with seating for eight.

Jessica opened a door in the corner of the kitchen and found a fully stocked pantry with shelves of canned and dry foods, and a built-in wine cellar with differing temperatures for reds and whites. A laundry area with a washer, dryer, ironing board and clothes steamer was set up in an alcove along with a small bathroom containing a commode, shower stall and vanity. She left the pantry, returned to the kitchen and stared out the window at the river separating New York from New Jersey.

"How do you like it?" asked the familiar deep, drawling voice behind her.

Jessica had lost track of time when staring out the window. She turned to find Sawyer standing at the far end of kitchen holding Bootsy under his arm like a football. "It's beautiful, and you're right."

His eyebrows lifted. "About what?"

"It's definitely larger than a studio apartment."

He set Bootsy down. "Just a little." Sawyer extended his hand. "Come, let me show you your bedroom."

She took the proffered hand and followed him up a curving staircase covered in plush sand-colored carpeting. Jessica wanted to chide him for being so self-deprecating. Sawyer's loft was equal to the square footage of five Manhattan studio apartments.

"I hope Bootsy doesn't have an accident and ruin your floors."

Sawyer squeezed her fingers. "If he does then it's no big deal. No home can ever be completely child- or pet-proofed."

"Who decorated your place?" she asked when they stepped onto the second-story landing.

"Unlike you, I had to hire a professional." Jessica followed Sawyer down a wide hall, stopping at a door opposite a credenza with a grouping of commemorative Waterford sports-team paperweights. He opened the door, stepping aside for her to precede him. "You'll sleep here, while I'm down at the end of the hall on the left."

Jessica was momentarily stunned with the space where she would sleep. The monochromatic color on the first level was repeated in the bedroom, where a queen-size bed upholstered in Ultrasuede took center stage, the room appearing camera-ready for an *Architectural Digest* layout.

"I think I'll take a bath."

"Take your time. It's going to be a while before we eat. I'll bring up your bag, and then I'm going to shower and shave before I walk Bootsy."

"What's on the menu?" she asked.

"Tonight Sawyer Ristorante is offering a cold seafood antipasto and wine, followed with an entrée of grilled lamb rib chops and asparagus wrapped in goat cheese, dates and prosciutto. We'll also serve gelato and cappuccino for dessert."

"It sounds delicious. Does Sawyer Ristorante have a dress code?" she teased.

"We usually require our guests to dress a little less casual on date night." He pulled her into a close embrace, brushing a kiss over her parted lips. "Thank you for being here."

Rising on tiptoe, Jessica pressed closer. "Thank you for being *you*," she whispered, deepening the kiss.

And at that moment she questioned if what she was beginning to feel for the man holding her to his heart was nothing more than infatuation. Going on tiptoe, her arms circling his neck, she held on to him as if he were a lifeline. His arms tightened around her waist, effortlessly lifting her off her feet as he devoured her mouth like a man deprived of food. Her heart pounded against her ribs when she detected the growing bulge in his groin pressing against her middle. The hardness elicited a pulsing between her thighs at the same time she tried to get even closer. Jessica wanted so much for him to make love to her as she went completely pliant in his arms.

Sawyer felt Jessica's breasts grow heavy against his chest and he knew he had to stop before he would not be able to. Reaching up, he gently pulled her arms from around his neck as he reluctantly ended the kiss. Her breathing was as labored as his and he managed to put a modicum of space between them.

Turning on his heel, walking stiffly and gritting his teeth while struggling not to press his hand against the throbbing bulge in his groin, he swallowed a moan of pleasure. The erection wasn't a reminder of how long it'd been since he'd slept with a woman but how much he wanted to lie between Jessica's thighs. And he could not remember a time when he wanted to make love to a woman as much as he did at that moment.

Sawyer retraced his steps, picking up her luggage as he tried not to think of the woman with whom he would share his home for at least a week. He found himself in a quandary because he had to decide whether he would spend the next year in New York or Wickham Falls.

Chapter Eleven

Jessica lost track of time as she reclined in the tub and pulsing jets of water massaged her body. She forced herself to get out, dry off and slather her favorite perfume crème cologne over her body. She had just slipped into a pair of four-inch black silk peep-toe booties when she heard a light tapping on the bedroom door and Sawyer announcing that it was time to eat.

"I'm ready," she called out, walking to the door. She opened it to find Sawyer staring at her as he had done when she saw him for the first time. Then she thought it had been curiosity but now she recognized it as lust. And there was no doubt her eyes reflected the same when she couldn't pull her gaze away from his clean-shaven jaw and the thick hair brushed off his forehead. He had exchanged his rugby shirt, jeans and running shoes for a blue shirt that was the exact color of his eyes, black tailored slacks and leather slip-ons.

He smiled. "You look and smell incredible."

She gave him a demure smile. "Thank you." She had tried on two outfits before deciding on the de rigueur little black dress, ending at her knees. Each time she inhaled, a swell of breasts was visible above the revealing neckline. He offered his arm and Jessica looped hers over his as they made their way down the staircase.

The scene that met her rendered her momentarily mute once she stepped off the last stair. The man she trusted *and* with whom she found herself falling in love was an unabashed romantic. The dimmed lights and subtle illumination from the electric fireplace reflected off all light surfaces. The melodious voice of Michael Bublé that flowed from wireless speakers set the mood for an intimate setting; her gaze shifted to the vase of fresh flowers on the dining room table set for two.

"I think I'm going to enjoy sharing date night with you. Soft lighting, music, flowers. How very romantic," Jessica crooned.

Sawyer pulled her into a close embrace and rested his chin on the top of her head. "That's because you deserve to wined and dined. Come with me to the kitchen where we can begin our date night with a toast."

She sat on the stool at the cooking island watching Sawyer as he expertly uncorked a bottle of rosé and filled two wineglasses with the pale pink liquid. "Are you certain you don't want me to help you?" Jessica had to ask even though he appeared to have everything under control. To go along with the asparagus there was a platter of marinated lamb rib chops with minced garlic, sea salt and freshly ground black pepper, drizzled with olive oil. She couldn't believe he'd put dinner together so quickly.

He glanced up, giving her a quick smile. "Thanks, but no thanks." He handed her one of the flutes. "For friendship and beyond."

Jessica touched her glass to his. "For friendship," she repeated. "Are you certain you weren't a short-order cook in another life?" she teased.

"Very certain. When I called in the grocery order I had the guy in the deli department season the meat and wrap the asparagus. They had all the ingredients for the antipasto on hand, so that saved time."

Her gaze shifted to the platter of cold seafood. "You like to cook." Her question was a statement.

Sawyer met her eyes. "I like experimenting with different dishes. I don't think I'll ever be as good as you, but I try."

Resting an elbow on the countertop, Jessica cradled her chin on the heel of one hand. "I admire a man who doesn't have to rely on a woman or women to take care of him."

His smile vanished, replaced by a frown. "Men who rely on women to take care of them aren't what I think of as grown men."

Her eyebrows lifted slightly. "What are they?"

"Parasites."

"That's a really strong word."

"There are a few other adjectives I could use, but I'm trying to stop cussing around you. Unless a man is physically, mentally or emotionally unable to care for himself, then he shouldn't look for a woman to give what he needs to survive day to day. For example if we were married, then you'd never have to worry about my not taking care of you financially or emotionally. And the same would go for our children."

Jessica's fingers tightened around the stem of the glass. She forced a smile that did not reach her eyes. "You haven't proposed marriage, nor have we slept together, and you have us married with children."

Raising his glass, Sawyer leaned closer. "If I did propose, could you see yourself becoming my wife?"

She took a sip of wine, holding it in her mouth before letting it slide down her throat. "You're crazy, Sawyer!"

A slow smile parted his firm lips. "Am I, Jessica?" He put the glass to his mouth and took a deep swallow before setting it down. Resting both elbows on the countertop, he gave her a long, penetrating stare. "I don't think so. I'm not a novice when it comes to women. I don't know what there is about you, but you…you tug at my heart." Rounding the cooking island, Sawyer gently eased her off the stool and into his arms. He caught her chin in his hand, forcing her to look at him. "Do you have any idea of who you are? You're intelligent, beautiful," he continued, not giving her a chance to answer his question, "hypnotically sexy and undeniably feminine."

A slight frown furrowed her forehead. "What are you talking about?"

"I've watched you interact with my family and your friends and I keep telling myself you can't be that patient or generous."

"You make it sound as if I'm perfect, Sawyer."

Lowering his head, he pressed his mouth to her parted lips. "Perfect for me."

Jessica's fingers circled his wrists, holding him fast. "That's called infatuation. In other words, your hormones are going into overdrive."

"It's more than that, Jess. If it were hormones then I

never would've invited you to stay with me. Women I sleep with never stay beyond one night."

Jessica found she couldn't think straight with him being so close. Her gaze lingered on his mouth. "Is it," she whispered, "that I'm different from the others?"

He slowly shook his head. "No, babe. You are the exception, because you're nothing like them. In other words, you are very, very special to me. Does that surprise you?"

A smile trembled over her parted lips as she eased out of his loose embrace and took another sip of wine, her eyes meeting Sawyer's over the rim.

Since she met Sawyer it was as if Gregory had never existed. Sawyer was mature, forthcoming and confident—qualities she admired in a man. But then, it wasn't fair for her to compare a twenty-year-old college student to a successful thirty-three-year-old entrepreneur.

"No, it doesn't, because you're very special to me."

Over dinner, Jessica and Sawyer talked about movies they had given thumb's up or down as nightfall shrouded the island of Manhattan.

Jessica touched the napkin to the corners of her mouth before placing it beside her plate. "That was delicious." She hadn't lied. The lamb chops and asparagus were perfectly broiled.

"What do you want to eat tomorrow?" Sawyer asked.

She pressed her hand against her middle. "I'm as full as a tick and you're already asking me about tomorrow. It seems as if every time we're together we eat."

His smile faded at the same time his lids came down as if to conceal his innermost thoughts from her. "I can think of other things we can do together that have nothing to do with eating."

Jessica's pulse quickened when he glanced up at her after a pregnant silence. "Are you referring to us making love to each other?"

Sawyer flashed a tender smile. "No, babe. I wasn't thinking of that, even though it has crossed my mind on a few occasions."

She felt an invisible wire pulling them closer, binding them together until they'd become one. "What do you have in mind?"

"I want to take you away to a private island for a couple of weeks where we can live like hedonists and the only people we'll see will be a valet, a personal chef and a masseur because I know how much you detest crowds when vacationing."

"That's sounds very tempting." Jessica had viewed travel programs featuring private islands and she'd found herself living vicariously through the host.

"Say yes and I'll make it happen."

Jessica exhaled an audible breath. "It's too late for that to happen this summer because I'm not certain exactly when Taryn's coming down. She says she'll probably spend about a week with me. After she leaves I have to prepare for the new school year."

Sawyer ran his forefinger down the length of her nose before pressing his thumb to her parted lips. "What about the Christmas recess? It would be the perfect time for you to get away from the cold weather." He stood up and began clearing the table.

"What are you? A genie granting wishes?"

"Wrong, beautiful. This time you didn't ask me to take you anywhere. You going away with me to a private island has been my fantasy from the first time I laid eyes on you. I didn't know what I truly wanted in a woman until I met you."

A hint of a smile trembled over her lips. "You're really laying it on thick, aren't you?" she said cynically.

Sawyer's expression changed, becoming a mask of stone. "You really think I'm pissing against the wind."

"You don't have to put it so bluntly."

He glared at her. "I could've said a lot more things a little more raw for your delicate ears, princess," he spat out angrily. "Do you want to hear them?"

"No, thank you," she retorted. "I think we better change the subject before we both say something we'll regret." They stared at each other, neither willing to yield while Jessica realized the man with whom she'd found herself falling in love was just as stubborn as or even more obstinate than she.

She was the first to break the stalemate when she said, "Come dance with me." It was the first night they would spend together and she did not want to begin it arguing over minutiae. Her invitation to dance together dissolved the chill between them as Sawyer bowed gracefully, reached for her hand and led her into the living room.

He pulled her into a close embrace as they danced to the melodious voice of Sam Smith singing "Stay with Me." The heartfelt lyrics tugged at her heart as she struggled not to let the tears filling her eyes fall.

"Sawyer."

"What is it, babe?"

Jessica's heart beat like a trip-hammer against her ribs. "I need you."

He stopped in midstep. "How?"

She inhaled a breath and then let it out slowly at the

same time his moist breath feathered over her forehead. "I... I need you to make love to me." The words that lay in her heart were out and she couldn't retract them.

His hands moved up, cradling her face. "Are you certain that's what you want?"

The seconds ticked off as she struggled to keep her knees from shaking. "Very certain."

Her hands came up, covering his. Desire coursed through her body, settling in her breasts and downward to her core. Jessica smothered a gasp when she felt Sawyer's erection against her thighs.

The two words were barely off her tongue when Sawyer swept her up in his arms, carrying her to the staircase. He took the stairs two at a time, long strides covering the distance from the living room to his bedroom in under a minute. He had not bothered to close the wall-to-wall drapes and the light of a full moon cast an eerie glow over the king-sized bed.

He placed her on the bed, his body following hers down, and she was certain he could hear the runaway beating of her heart against his chest. Sawyer pressed his face to the column of her neck. "If there's something you don't want me to do, then you must tell me."

Jessica wanted to tell him to stop talking and make love to her. She closed her eyes and forced herself to breathe deeply and slowly as Sawyer undressed her, his hands moving seemingly in slow motion. He began with her shoes, dress and bra, and then stopped when it came to removing her bikini panties.

Sawyer slipped off the bed, the whisper of fabric grazing his skin as he undressed. Sounds were magnified when he opened a drawer in the bedside table. Seconds later she recognized the sound of a condom packet being opened. How could she have forgotten about protection when Sawyer had verbalized he wasn't ready to become a father any more than she wanted an unplanned pregnancy?

He returned to the bed, the heat of his muscled physique enveloping her as he relieved her of the delicate scrap of silk concealing her nakedness. Jessica hadn't realized that she was holding her breath until after he pulled her into a tender embrace where her nude body touched his and made her blatantly aware of the differences.

"Sawyer?"

"Yes, babe?"

"You're going to have to show me how to please you."

Sawyer pressed a kiss to her forehead. "You don't have to do anything. You please me just by existing."

That was not what she meant, but he didn't give her the opportunity to explain herself as he took possession of her mouth in a slow, drugging kiss that produced a rush of moisture between her thighs. His mouth moved lower, to her breasts, and she was lost in a maelstrom of desire that completely shattered her dammed-up sexuality.

Waves of passion shook Jessica until she couldn't stop her legs from shaking. Sawyer suckled her breasts, worshipping them, and the moans she sought to suppress escaped her parted lips. His tongue circled her nipples, leaving them hard, erect and throbbing, his teeth tightening on the turgid tips at the same time she felt a violent spasm grip her womb.

"Sawyer!" His name exploded from her mouth as he inched down her body, holding her hips firmly. Shock supplanted passion once Jessica realized where he'd buried his face. His hot breath seared the moist curls, and she went limp, unable to protest further or think of anything except the pleasure her lover offered her. She registered a series of breathless sighs, not realizing they were her own moans of physical satisfaction. Eyes closed, head thrown back, lips parted, back arched, she reveled in the sensations that took her beyond herself. Then it began, rippling little tremors increasing and becoming more volatile as they sought to escape.

Sawyer heard Jessica's breathing come in long, surrendering moans, and he quickly moved up her trembling limbs and eased his erection inside her at the same time he felt a slight resistance. "I'm hurting you?"

"Not enough for you to stop. Please, Sawyer, don't leave me like this."

He gritted his teeth as he eased his penis inside her, inch by agonizing inch, until he was buried up to the root in the hot, moist, tight flesh pulsing around his own. He began moving in a slow, measured rhythm wherein they were in perfect harmony with each other. Reaching down, he cupped her hips in his hands, lifting her higher and permitting deeper penetration. Jessica assisted him, increasing her own pleasure when she wound her legs around his waist.

Sawyer's heat, hardness and carnal sensuality had awakened the dormant sexuality of her body and Jessica responded to the seduction of his passion as hers rose higher and higher until it exploded in an awesome, vibrating liquid fire, scorching her mind and leaving her convulsing in ecstasy. She had not returned from her own free-fall flight when she heard Sawyer's groan of satisfaction against her ear as he quickened his movements and then collapsed heavily on her body. They lay motionless, savoring the aftermath of a shared, sweet fulfillment.

He reversed their positions, bringing her with him until she lay sprawled over his body, her legs resting between his. "Are you certain I didn't hurt you, sweetheart?"

"No," she drawled, placing tiny kisses on his throat and over his shoulder.

"I know you—"

Jessica stopped his words when she placed her fingertips over his lips. "I'm all right, Sawyer."

"Is there anything I did you didn't like?"

She hesitated. "No."

After the initial shock had faded when Sawyer put his face between her legs, Jessica felt as if she was lifted outside of herself and transported to a place where she had never been. Waves of ecstasy had throbbed through her, rendering her as helpless as a newborn. Sawyer wasn't merely filling a physical need, he'd managed to tear down the wall she had put up not to trust a man.

Sawyer breathed a kiss over her ear. "I'm glad, because I love making love with you."

His right hand moved over her bare hip, caressing the silken flesh. Jessica had no idea how sensuous her voice sounded in the dark. He drew a deep breath and luxuriated in the intoxicating fragrance of her perfume stamped on his flesh like a permanent tattoo.

Closing his eyes, Sawyer tightened his hold on her slender body. He was in love with Jessica. He didn't know when it happened, but he had fallen inexorably in love with her. And now that she was a part of his existence, he had no intention of letting her walk out of his life.

"I have to get up," he whispered softly, "and get rid of the condom. Try not to run away."

Jessica's sensual laugh filled the bedroom. "I'll be here when you come back, because I'm not good at a one-night stand."

Reversing their positions again he kissed her passionately. "Love you."

It wasn't until he stood in the bathroom staring at his reflection in the mirror that Sawyer recalled he had admitted to Jessica that he loved her. Although spoken glibly, the admission had come from his heart. He returned to the bed, slipping in beside Jessica and pulling her against his body. They lay together like spoons before both succumbed to a comforting sleep of sated lovers.

Turning on her right side, Jessica inhaled the lingering scent of her lover's aftershave. The imprint of his head was still visible on the pillow next to hers. Somehow he had gotten out of bed without waking her. The last thing she remembered before falling asleep was Sawyer's admission that he loved her. Had he said it because he really did love her, or it was what he thought she wanted to hear after their making love with each other? Jessica closed her eyes, chiding herself from attempting to overanalyze what she had shared with Sawyer. Why, she thought, couldn't she just let everything unfold naturally and enjoy their time together?

She opened her eyes and peered at the clock on the bedside table. It was minutes before seven. It was past time she took Bootsy out for his morning walk.

Galvanized into action, she swung her legs over the side of the bed. Ever mindful of her nakedness despite sharing her body with Sawyer, she peered down the hallway and, finding it empty, sprinted to her bedroom. She had to shower, dress and take care of Bootsy.

Twenty minutes later Jessica descended the staircase and walked into the kitchen. The door to the pantry stood open and when she glanced in she found Bootsy's crate empty and his bowls filled with fresh food and water. She turned and saw the note attached to the refrigerator door with a computer-mouse magnet. Sawyer and Bootsy had gone out for a walk.

She retraced her steps and returned to the bedroom to make up the bed. If she'd had any uncertainty about falling in love with Sawyer it had fled after their lovemaking as she recalled the smoldering passion that made her want him even now. She was in love and had fallen in love with a man who made her laugh, feel ultrafeminine and look forward to spending as much time with him as possible before he left Wickham Falls at the end of the summer.

She lingered long enough to stare out the window. A haze hung over the Hudson River and obscured the New Jersey shoreline. Now she knew why Sawyer preferred living in New York. The spacious duplex was conducive to entertaining and relaxation while offering incredible views of the river. Her sock-covered feet were silent as she went back to the kitchen to brew a pot of coffee.

The elevator doors opened and Sawyer set Bootsy on the floor. When he'd left the loft earlier that morning his intent was to walk along the pier then pick up the Sunday *Times*, but halfway through the first mile Bootsy sat down and refused to move.

The aroma of brewing coffee wafted to his nostrils as he walked through the living room. "Honey, I'm home," he called out as he entered the kitchen, setting the newspaper on the countertop.

Jessica stood at the breakfast bar holding a carafe filled with steaming coffee. She flashed a shy smile. "Good morning."

He approached her, cupped her hips over a pair of body-hugging jeans and dropped a soft kiss on her mouth. "Good morning, babe."

Sawyer thought he'd imagined it, but Jessica looked different this morning. His eyes moved slowly over her bare face before noting her hair. She'd brushed it off her forehead. He wasn't disappointed when she put her arms around his neck and kissed his throat.

"Do you want a cup of coffee?"

"Yes, please. I need to wash my hands first."

Jessica eased out of his loose embrace and took two mugs from an overhead cabinet. "How was your walk?" she asked after he returned from the small bathroom and dried his hands on a paper towel.

"It was okay."

She glanced at him over her shoulder. "Just okay?"

"Bootsy got tired and I had to carry him. I must admit I got some strange looks. A woman told me to 'put that dog down and let him walk.'"

"What did you say?"

"Nothing. But I did want to tell her to mind her own damn business because I can do whatever I want with my dog."

She halted filling a mug and gave him an incredulous stare. "Bootsy's now your dog?"

Sawyer ruffled her short hair. "Now that we're officially a couple, he's *our* dog."

Jessica smiled, wordlessly validating their relationship.

"What's on today's agenda?" she asked.

"I hadn't planned anything. What do you want to do?"

"If you don't mind I'd like to stay indoors and relax."

His arms encircled her waist, one hand resting at the small of her back. Sawyer had hoped she would say that. The refrigerator was stocked with enough fresh food for several days; the video library with classic and current award-winning films and TV miniseries would keep them entertained for hours. He picked her up, smiling when he felt her eyelashes brushing against his cheek.

"I'd hoped you would say that."

"I finally figured out where I want to go while we're here."

He met her eyes. They were shimmering with excitement. "Where?"

Jessica made a sexy pout. "I'd like to go to Coney Island to ride the Cyclone and eat Nathan's hot dogs. Then the next day I want to go to Brooklyn again and walk over the bridge to Manhattan where we can spend the rest of the day at the South Street Seaport before walking up to Greenwich Village and eating pizza in Little Italy."

Sawyer bit back a smile, wondering if Jessica knew how much walking they would do that day. "Where else, babe?"

"If we can fit it in, then I'd like to visit the American Museum of Natural History. The last time I came to New York I didn't see half of what I wanted to see here."

"I suppose you want to celebrate the Fourth here, rather than in The Falls?" he asked.

Celebrating the Fourth of July holiday had become the mother of all celebrations for the residents of Wickham Falls. There was a parade along Main Street that included the high school and middle school marching bands, cheerleaders, sports teams, the Sweet Potato Queen riding on the Chamber of Commerce float, Boy and Girl Scout troops and veterans in uniforms ranging from WWII to the present parading with the local American Legion and VFW.

"I have many more years to celebrate the holiday in The Falls, but I'm not certain when I'll get to see the Macy's fireworks show again."

"You can always come back and stay with me anytime you want."

Jessica's eyebrows lifted slightly. "You say that now because you don't have a wife but if you did, do you actually think another woman would welcome your former lover with open arms to sleep under the same roof as her husband or lover?"

"That's not going to happen."

"Because you say so, Sawyer?"

"Because I'd never disrespect a woman like that. If you were to come here you'd never have to concern yourself with my being involved with another woman."

Leaning closer, Jessica kissed his stubble. "You're definitely a keeper."

"So are you," he confirmed as he took her mouth in a slow, surprisingly gentle kiss. The kiss ended with them both breathing heavily. No further words were needed

as Sawyer silently vowed that Jessica would become
the last woman in his life, because since meeting her
he didn't want another woman. She fulfilled everything
he wanted and needed in a life partner.

Chapter Twelve

Spending Sunday with Jessica offered Sawyer a glimpse of what their lives would be like if they were married. Although they did not make love again, he felt more connected to her than with any other woman in his past. They read the Sunday paper, cooked together and after dinner laughed uncontrollably while watching *Tower Heist*.

Sunday had been their day of rest, while Monday was about business as he was shown into his financial manager's office in a Park Avenue skyscraper overlooking Grand Central Terminal. He shook the proffered hand. "Thanks for making time to meet with me." Adam Novak had delayed his vacation to set up the meeting.

"I always make time for my prime clients." He gestured to a chair at the small round table. "Please have a seat."

Sawyer had promised Jessica he would secure funding for the grant before the start of the upcoming school year and that would become a possibility with Adam's assistance. He'd sent Adam an email, attaching the grant application.

Conservatively dressed with cropped graying hair, Adam looked as if he'd stepped off the *Mad Men* set. He handed Sawyer a folder. "Sign next to the red flags and I'll transfer the funds to your new charity. Let me know when you want me to forward the check to the school district along with a copy of the grant application."

Sawyer scrawled his signature on a half dozen pages before pulling out his cell phone and tapping on the calendar. He wanted the district to receive the monies before the beginning of the upcoming school year, which would give them enough time to interview and hire a full-time technology teacher and IT person.

"July tenth."

"Consider it done. I'll have my assistant email you copies of what you've signed. You should get them sometime this afternoon." Adam laced his fingers together. "You're doing what I recommend some of my clients do. Donate to a worthy cause."

"Do they?" Sawyer asked.

"You're the second. How does it feel to be a philanthropist?"

"I'm hardly a philanthropist. It's more like giving back."

Sawyer stood up, Adam following suit, and extended his hand. "Thanks again for everything."

"It's always my pleasure, Sawyer."

Twenty minutes after arriving at the investment firm Sawyer walked out into the bright morning Manhattan sunlight. He did not want to think of the donation as a personal triumph for the woman with whom he'd fallen in love, but for the school district which prepared him for what he had become.

Instead of taking a taxi or the subway from Grand Central he decided to walk back to his Chelsea neighborhood. He became a tourist while stopping to window shop along Fifth Avenue. He walked into the Mikimoto boutique when he recalled the pearls Jessica had worn Friday night.

A salesman approached him. "Good afternoon. May I help you, sir?"

"Yes. I'd like to get a gift for my girlfriend." *Girlfriend*. The word had slipped easily off his tongue.

The middle-aged, bespectacled, well-dressed man smiled and extended his hand. "I'm Bellamy, and you've come to the right place. I doubt if there's a woman on the planet who wouldn't like pearls as a gift. Which type are you interested in?"

Sawyer's gaze swept over several strands in varying shades. "I'm not certain." He listened intently as Bellamy described the differences between Akoya, conch, and baroque, black, white and golden sea pearls. "I think I like the golden best." The contrast of the perfectly matched gold-hued pearls against Jessica's complexion would be spectacular.

Bellamy pressed his palms together. "Excellent choice. The deeper golden colors are the most coveted of all pearls." He directed Sawyer to a showcase with pearls in sizes of nine millimeters and higher, selecting a strand as overhead light shimmered off the baubles, giving them the appearance of liquid gold. "Here's an exquisite graduated strand. The larger pearls are almost fourteen millimeters and the smaller a tad over ten. It's seventeen inches in length and the diamond clasp is eighteen-karat yellow gold."

Three quarters of an hour later, Sawyer reached into the breast pocket of his jacket for his credit card as Bellamy totaled his purchase. He'd selected a strand of pearls and matching earrings. He pulled out his cell phone as he waited for the man to process the sale and sent Jessica a text message.

Sawyer: Do you want to go to Coney Island this afternoon?

He stared at the screen, waiting for her reply.

Jessica: Hell yeah!

Sawyer: I'll be home soon.

Jessica: OK

His thumbs paused on the screen.

Sawyer: Love you

Jessica: Love you back

Returning the phone to the pocket of his jacket, Sawyer thought about her response. Jessica hadn't said she loved him, but her typing the word was enough to buoy his spirits that there was hope they could possibly share a future. And if he proposed marriage and Jessica agreed, then they had to decide where they would live.

Sawyer wondered whether he could ask her to give up her home and move to New York, but he was now a New Yorker in every sense of the word, and his involvement in Enigma4For4 was critical for the future of the company. He chided himself for mentally fast-forwarding his relationship with Jessica.

Bellamy gave him back the credit card and a shopping bag with the pearls. "Thank you, Mr. Middleton. I'm certain the lady will be quite pleased with your purchase."

"I certain she will," he said confidently. He planned to give Jessica the pearls as a gift for her securing the grant.

Jessica inhaled a deep breath of salt air as Sawyer assisted her out of the Jeep. A rush of adrenaline made her feel like a little girl as they walked closer to the historic amusement park.

She glanced up at Sawyer when he reached for her hand. "I love the smell of the ocean."

He squeezed her fingers. "I don't know what it is, but food always seems to taste better in the sea air."

"Even though I'm hungry enough to go through an entire smorgasbord, I want to ride the Cyclone first. Are you going on with me?" she asked Sawyer.

"I'll go, but only if you promise to hold my hand if I start to cry."

Jessica gave him an incredulous stare. "You're kidding me, aren't you?" she asked.

"No."

"You've never ridden a roller coaster?"

"I have," he admitted, "but it was somewhat traumatic."

"Traumatic how?"

"The moment I got off I tossed my cookies."

"How old were you?"

"Six."

Jessica rested a comforting hand on his forearm. "You don't have to go on if you don't want."

"I do want to," Sawyer said, grinning from ear to ear.

It took her at least ten seconds to realize she had been had. "You were only teasing!" she said accusingly.

Sawyer's shoulders shook as he tried not to laugh. "I'm sorry, babe, but I couldn't resist teasing you. You should've seen your face."

She narrowed her eyes at him. "I'm going to pay you back for that."

Dipping his head, he brushed a kiss over her parted lips. "Sorry."

A beat passed. "Apology accepted." There was no way she could remain angry with the man with whom she was falling in love. Jessica waited on line as he purchased the tickets for a ride on the National Historic Landmark wooden roller coaster.

Jessica became a child again as she felt the swooping feeling in her stomach as the roller coaster roared down the track, the click-clack of wood establishing a rhythm she would remember for all time. After the ride she and Sawyer headed toward Nathan's. Again, there were long lines as crowds waited to buy the legendary hot dogs. She had to admit to Sawyer that the frankfurter's reputation as the best tasting in the country was not a fluke. They spent the afternoon strolling along the boardwalk before going down to the beach. Sawyer took off his shoes, rolled up his jeans to the knee and waded into the ocean.

Jessica followed suit, gasping aloud when the cold, gray water rushed over her feet and legs. "It's colder than I thought it would be."

Sawyer caught her hand, pulling her farther into the ocean. "If we'd brought suits we could've gone swimming."

She shook her head. Despite the chilly water temperature there were swimmers braving the pounding waves and rough surf.

"No!" she screamed when Sawyer scooped up a handful of water and splashed her. Not willing to let him get away with wetting her, Jessica lunged at his knees, the momentum knocking him off balance so he went down in the surf. Seconds later she found herself sitting beside him when he pulled her down. They splashed each other until both were breathing heavily.

Sitting on the beach, Jessica laughed until she struggled to catch her breath. Although wet and chilled, she could not remember when she'd enjoyed herself more. Hanging out with Sawyer made her feel as if she did not have a care in the world, and when she thought about it, she had to admit her life was as close to perfect as it could get.

Always the pragmatist, Jessica knew the time she would spend with Sawyer was not of long duration; she did not regret it because she realized people would come into and out of her life—some who would be instrumental in changing her and others who would make her aware of her strengths and weaknesses. Making love with Sawyer had become a catharsis—a purging of the distrust of men she'd carried within her consciousness for far too long.

Her laughter faded completely when he pulled her up

to stand, his gaze fixed on her chest. Glancing down, Jessica realized the outlines of her distended nipples were clearly visible through the wet white T-shirt and silk bra. Pulling the damp fabric away from her body, she met Sawyer's eyes.

"I can't walk around like this."

Combing his fingers through his hair, Sawyer placed his soaked cap on his head. "You're right. There's a shop not far from here selling T-shirts and souvenirs." He draped an arm over her shoulders and he pulled her close. "I'm sorry about getting you soaked."

Smiling, Jessica tilted her chin. "I'm not. It was fun."

The souvenir shop carried everything from picture postcards to various articles of clothing and figurines extolling Brooklyn, Coney Island and New York City. She emerged from the shop's dressing room in a pair of shorts and a gray sweatshirt with the Brooklyn Stand Up logo.

"Aren't you going to change into something dry?" she asked Sawyer.

"No." He rested his hands over his chest. "I don't think anyone would be interested in staring at my ta-tas. Yours, however, are quite easy on the eyes. But for my eyes only."

Jessica was helpless to stop the rush of heat flooding her cheeks. She had no comeback. They had shared a shower earlier that morning while exploring each other's bodies but stopping short of making love.

Looping her arm through his, she gave him a long, penetrating stare. "The day has been perfect, but I want to go home—now."

They left Brooklyn, and the ride back to Manhattan was accomplished in complete silence, each seemingly lost in their own musings. After seeing to Bootsy, Sawyer and Jessica retreated to separate bathrooms to shower.

He was lying in bed, his back supported by a pile of pillows and arms outstretched, when Jessica ran, jumped into his embrace and kissed him. He tasted toothpaste and mouthwash on her breath as his tongue slipped into her mouth. She went compliant before relaxing under his oral onslaught. He released the towel draped around her body, dropping it on the floor.

"You don't know how I wanted to touch you when I saw you in that wet T-shirt," he whispered hoarsely. After having sampled the sensual and physical delights of her body, Sawyer discovered himself addicted to her smell, taste and touch.

Jessica breathed a kiss under his ear. "You can touch me now."

He covered her mouth with his in a soft, caressing kiss. "Where?"

"Everywhere."

Her voice had dropped to a lower octave, sending shivers up his back as he became a sculptor, his hands and mouth mapping every dip and curve of Jessica's body. His mouth closed over her firm breasts, suckling and teasing them with his teeth at the same time one hand slid up her thighs; his thumb pressed against her clitoris and caused her to arch off the bed. He wanted to go slowly, but the dampness dotting his fingers and the soft moans coming from Jessica caused the blood to rush so quickly to his penis that he suddenly felt lightheaded.

Sawyer's hands were shaking when he reached for the condom on the bedside table and attempted to slip it on. Lowering his body, he kissed her again, summoning a tenderness he hadn't known he had. Making love with Jessica was different only because he was not the same man he had been before meeting her.

Jessica clung to Sawyer, his kisses warm and comforting. With each brush of his lips a delicious shudder rippled through her body, bringing with it a powerful desire to surrender all of herself. "Love me, please," she pleaded.

"Open your legs for me, baby."

She complied, parting her knees as Sawyer's hardened sex pushed into her; she moaned softly at the slow, intense penetration. Flames of desire rose quickly, overlapping her soft moans as her taut flesh stretched with each inch until he was fully sheathed. Then, in a rhythm that was as timeless as the beginning of creation, she offered him all of herself, holding nothing back.

Sawyer established a slow, deliberate thrusting as Jessica rose to meet him. Anchoring his hands under her hips, he held her fast, increasing the cadence, his hips moving with the velocity and power of a piston. Her gasps and soft moans served to make the heat in his loins even more intense. He lost himself in the moment and the love flowing from the woman under him, not feeling the bite of her fingernails on his back. What he was aware of was the gurgling sounds coming from her throat that erupted into an unrestrained primal scream sending him over a precipice where he surrendered all he had and was to the woman whom he knew he would love forever. They climaxed simultaneously, experiencing a shared free fall that made them one with each other.

They lay entwined, breathing heavily, waiting for their respiration to slow while enjoying the lingering pulsing sensations. He did not want to move. However, Sawyer was forced to when he withdrew from Jessica and went to discard the condom. When he returned to the bed he found her lying on her side, her back to him. He lay beside her and within minutes Morpheus claimed both.

Pulling her into a close embrace, Sawyer planted a whisper of a kiss on Jessica's forehead. The time they had spent in New York had ended all too soon. "I'll call you tomorrow."

She watched his departing figure as he slipped behind the wheel of the Jeep and drove away. The wonderful week was over. They'd returned to Wickham Falls to pick up where they left off before their sleeping together. A hint of a smile tilted the corners of her mouth when Bootsy howled as Sawyer sped away. The two had bonded, the puppy following Sawyer everywhere while whining incessantly to be picked up.

The week in New York had become a fairy-tale experience wherein she'd managed to visit all of the places on her *must-see* list, including watching the Fourth of July fireworks from the loft's rooftop.

Jessica clapped her hands. "Come inside, Bootsy. It's time to go to bed."

Smothering a yawn, she locked the door and headed for the staircase. After a bath, she pulled on a cotton nightgown and slipped into bed alone, marveling at how quickly she'd gotten used to sharing a bed with Sawyer. She closed her eyes, and after tossing and turning for a while, she finally fell asleep.

* * *

After dropping Jessica off Sawyer paced the length of the porch like a caged large cat because he was too wound up to go to bed. He knew some of his uneasiness stemmed from his increasingly deep feelings for Jessica, and against all of his protestations that he wasn't ready to marry, he wanted to claim her as his wife and eventually the mother of their children.

He knew purchasing the pearls had been based on impulse, yet they represented more to him than just a gift to a woman with whom he'd fallen in love. The pearls would become heirloom pieces that could be passed down from mother to daughter and eventually granddaughter. He found himself thinking about future generations when he wasn't certain whether Jessica would even agree to marry him.

He was still pacing when his cell phone chimed that he had a text. Reaching into the pocket of his jeans and taking out the phone, he read the message, his eyebrows lifting slightly.

Thom: Need you in New York ASAP to look over space invaders game Joon and Erik worked on in their spare time.

Sawyer: Have Shirley make flight and ground transportation arrangements for tomorrow morning.

Thom: No problem. Safe travel.

Sawyer: Thanks

He held the phone, staring at the screen for a full minute, then sent a text to Jessica's phone alerting her that he had to return to New York to work on a project, and he wasn't certain when he would return. Sawyer had hoped to spend time with Jessica before her friend arrived. Opening the screen door, he went inside the house, and locked it and the inner door.

Chapter Thirteen

Jessica walked into the airport terminal. Taryn's plane was on the ground and her friend had sent her a text to meet her at baggage claim. Her friend had flown in from New York, while her lover had returned to New York.

The morning following her return from New York she'd turned on her cell phone to find the text from Sawyer. It was the first of daily texts sent at various hours during the day and night, and all contained the same three words: I miss you. He missed her and she missed him, too. She replied with one word: Ditto.

Jessica broke into a smile when she saw her former college roommate, hardly recognizing her without her ubiquitous braids. Taryn had begun wearing braids in college and the last time Jessica had seen her they were nearly waist length. Now, chemically straightened dark brown blunt-cut strands ending above her shoulders and held off her face with a narrow headband made her appear girlishly chic.

Standing five-ten in bare feet, Taryn always turned heads because with her delicate features and café au lait complexion most people mistook her for a model. She pulled a wheeled duffel with one hand and had looped a matching tote over the opposite shoulder.

The lines around Taryn's eyes crinkled when Jessica reached for the tote and pressed her cheek to her friend's. "Welcome to West Virginia, and thanks for coming."

"Thank you for inviting me." Taryn scrunched up her pert nose. "You're a real savior, Jess. I needed to get away because living with my parents, and now my grandmother, was working my last nerve. I think they forget I'm a grown-ass woman when they ask me what time I'm coming home. It's been years since I had a curfew."

"I love my parents dearly, but three thousand miles make our reunions all the more special."

"How are your parents?" Taryn asked as they made their way out of the terminal to the parking lot.

"They're still in Alaska."

"Good for them," Taryn remarked. "My mother's waiting for my dad to retire before going abroad, but that may change now that Grandma's living with us. Daddy says he'll pay someone to stay with his mother if they do decide to go away."

Jessica waited for Taryn to buckle her seat belt and then maneuvered out of the lot. Tapping a button on the steering wheel, she tuned to a satellite radio station featuring classic R & B. Within seconds they were singing at the top of their lungs, garnering strange glances from those in passing vehicles. Jessica laughed until tears streamed down her face as Taryn's voice cracked when she attempted to match Mariah Carey's five-octave range singing "Dreamlover."

"Please don't quit your day job," Jessica teased.

Taryn sobered. "That's exactly what I would like to do. I enjoy teaching but not the commute."

Jessica gave her a sidelong glance. "Couldn't you take the railroad instead of driving?"

"I would if I didn't have to take a bus once I get off the train. Now that I look back I realize I never should've given up my apartment. What did Billie Holiday say? 'God bless the child that's got his own.'"

Staring out the windshield, Jessica concentrated on the road. "Do you ever run into James at the gym?"

Taryn shook her head. "Once I moved back to Long Island I didn't renew my membership."

"Are you seeing anyone now?"

"No. What about you? Are you seeing anyone?"

"Yes," Jessica confirmed after a noticeable pause. She gave her friend a quick overview of her relationship with Sawyer, leaving out the intimate details.

"You say he's just here for the summer. Does that mean I'll get to meet him?" Taryn asked. Anticipation shimmered in her light brown eyes.

Jessica paused. "I'm not sure. Right now he's in New York working on a project and I don't know when he'll be back."

Taryn sobered. "I'm glad you met someone who makes you happy. You more than deserve it."

"Thanks. And you deserve to meet someone who isn't a jackass," Jessica countered, smiling.

"Jackass or horse's ass, I made a New Year's resolution not to date for a year only because I need to get my head together and figure out who Taryn Robinson is and what she wants or needs for her future. If I could, I'd like to go back to my college days when I looked after other people's children."

Jessica gave her a quick glance. "You really like being a nanny?" She and Taryn had shared an off-campus apartment in Washington, DC, and her roommate worked weekends as a babysitter to earn money to help cover her personal expenses.

"Not so much a nanny now as a governess employed to teach and train children in a private household."

"Are you really serious about leaving the classroom?"

"Quite serious."

"I know someone who's looking for someone to homeschool his daughters. You'd be perfect for the position." She told Taryn about Aiden looking for a live-in nanny.

Taryn grunted under her breath. "I don't think so, Jess. I really can't imagine myself living down here. I'm a big-city girl."

"So was I, my friend. Don't judge us country folks too harshly until you've been here awhile."

Taryn pulled her lower lip between her teeth, seemingly deep in thought. "Okay. I promise to keep an open mind. I have to admit, country life has been good for you."

"I love it," Jessica said truthfully.

She wanted to remind Taryn that she had options. She wasn't in a committed relationship, she didn't have children, she lived with her parents and was an experienced licensed educator, which meant she could pick up and relocate at a moment's notice.

They launched into a lively banter about their students, Taryn outdoing Jessica when it came to outrageous antics from her rambunctious kindergarteners. All conversation ended as Jessica maneuvered into the driveway to her home.

Bootsy greeted Taryn, sniffing her legs before rolling over on his back for a belly rub. "When your mama's not looking I'm going to hide you in my tote and take you back to New York. Then I'll dress you in haute couture before taking you to the doggie park," she crooned, stroking the puppy's belly.

"That's not going to happen," Jessica said, "because he's microchipped. Come upstairs with me and I'll show you your room."

Taryn stared at the furnishings in the open floor plan. "I never thought I'd say it, but I'm jealous of you."

A frown appeared between Jessica's eyes. "Why?"

"Look at your home. It's beautiful, while I'm sleeping in the same bedroom where I grew up."

Jessica hugged her friend. "Remember when you told me, 'This too shall pass'?"

Taryn forced a smile. "I do remember, and it's time I take my own advice. As soon as I shower and change we're going out for dinner. My treat."

Jessica waited for Taryn to grasp the handle of the duffel and led her up the staircase to the second story. She knew Taryn still hadn't recovered from the breakup with her boyfriend, because she'd fallen inexorably in love with James. Taryn had thought it serendipitous that she and James shared the same surname, believing they were fated to be soul mates.

"Fish or fowl?" Jessica asked, glancing over her shoulder.

"Neither. I want a big juicy steak smothered in onions and a loaded baked potato, followed by a slice of cheesecake and cappuccino."

"Stop it or you'll have me salivating," Jessica chided. "There's an incredibly good steakhouse off the interstate. I'll call and make reservations for eight."

Sawyer fell back on the bed at the same time a moan slipped past his lips. A tiredness he hadn't experienced in a very long time weighed him down like a leaded blanket, while he found it difficult to think clearly.

He groaned again. His shoulders were stiff from sitting in the same position for hours. It'd taken longer than projected to work out the bugs in the video game. If the graphics weren't so groundbreaking he would've suggested scrapping it. The computer-generated images were spectacular. Darius had come up with a concept for three games instead of one, and it took the engineers nearly two weeks to rewrite the code.

In his downtime he'd checked his emails. Rachel informed him their parents were returning to the mainland on July 28, while she planned to stay until two days before the first day of classes. She'd also attached photos of Colin and Dylan in the ocean on surfboards.

Sawyer had not realized he'd dozed off until he heard his cell phone's ringtone. Reaching across his body he swept it off the bedside table. "Hello."

"Did I wake you?"

He pushed into a sitting position. "I was just dozing."

Jessica's laugh came through the earpiece. "But it's one in the afternoon."

"I've been up for more than eighteen hours."

There came a pause on the other end. "I'm sorry—"

"Don't apologize, babe," he said, interrupting her. "It's good hearing your voice."

"I would've sent you a text, but what I have to tell you is too important to put in a text or email. The school district's business manager called to say he received a check for the grant. He said to tell you the school board members are meeting next week and they want to come up with a plan to honor one of their alumnae."

"We'll have to celebrate whenever I get back."

"You deserve the accolades, Sawyer, not me. The entire school district owes you, the committee owes you, and I owe you."

Sawyer eyelids fluttered as he struggled to stay awake. "I love you, Jessica."

A beat passed. "I love you, too."

His eyes opened and he went completely still, momentarily speechless. Had she said she loved him because she thought it was what he wanted to hear, or did she truly love him? "You say you owe me, and now I'm going to ask you to pay up." The silence on the other end of the line stretched out until he thought she had hung up.

"What do you want?" Jessica asked.

He heard trepidation in her voice. "I want you to marry me. We'll wait until Rachel and my folks get back from Hawaii. Hopefully by that time your parents will have returned from their Alaskan vacation."

There came another pause, this one more prolonged and pregnant than the first. "Look, Sawyer, you're half-asleep and we need to talk about this at another time."

Sawyer felt as if he'd won a small victory because she hadn't rejected his proposal. "You can't talk because you're not alone?"

"That's not it. It's just that I didn't expect you to ask me to marry you when you claim you're not ready for marriage."

"That's before I met you."

Jessica's husky laugh caressed his ear. "I must really have some powerful mojo to get a confirmed bachelor to change his mind so quickly."

"You ain't lying," he drawled.

Jessica laughed again. "Can we discuss this when you get back?"

"Of course we can, darling. I'm almost finished with my work here. I'll call you once I know for certain when I'll be coming home."

It took several attempts for Jessica to set the cordless phone in the charger. Her hands were shaking uncontrollably. She had just gotten a marriage proposal from a man she loved and she wasn't able to accept or reject it. By the time she rejoined Taryn on the patio she was back in control. Folding her body down to a webbed lawn chair positioned under an umbrella, she picked up the pitcher of sweet tea and topped off her glass.

"Are you all right?" Taryn asked, giving her a critical squint.

"Yes," she replied much too quickly.

Pulling her bare legs to her chest, Taryn wrapped her arms around her knees. Bootsy, who'd curled up against her legs, shifted until he lay on his belly. "Are you sure?"

"Yes. Why?"

"You looked like someone who can't find her winning Powerball ticket."

Jessica met Taryn's steady gaze. "Sawyer asked me to marry him."

Taryn sat up straight, her eyes growing wider with each passing second. "You're kidding?"

"No, I'm not," Jessica replied, shaking her head for emphasis.

"How long have you known him?"

"I met him for the first time two months ago, even though I feel as if I've known him much longer. I'm friends with his sister, and when Rachel would go on and on about her older brother being Mr. Wonderful I thought their relationship was a little creepy. But when I finally got to meet him I knew everything she'd said was true."

Swinging her legs over the chair, Taryn asked, "Are you in love with him?"

"Yes," Jessica admitted without hesitation.

"Are you going to accept his proposal?"

Jessica shook her head. "I don't know."

Taryn frowned. "What don't you know, Jess? Either you are or you're not."

A shiver of uneasiness swept over Jessica when she realized she shouldn't have broached the subject with Taryn, who would pressure her until she was forced to tell her everything. And not once had she pressured Taryn to give her the intimate details of her breakup with her live-in boyfriend.

"I'm indecisive." The two words were cutting and final. "I love him enough to become his wife, but things are happening much too quickly for me to make a decision right now."

"But didn't you tell me Sawyer's only going to be here until Labor Day? Are you really ready for a long-distance relationship?" Taryn asked.

"If our relationship can survive us living eight hundred miles apart, then it's meant to be."

Taryn averted her gaze. "You're indecisive and so am I."

Jessica's eyebrows lifted slightly. "What are you vacillating about?"

"After being here for more than a week, I realize I'm getting used to the quiet where I'm able to hear myself think. I suppose I'm so drawn into the hustle and bustle of a big city that I hadn't realized it's adding to my inability to let go of the past. If I move here, then I won't have to be reminded of James. Even though I can't forgive him for cheating on me with one of my friends, a part of me still loves him."

Jessica went completely still. Talk about true confessions. It was the first time Taryn had revealed the actual reason she and James broke up, but she also wanted to curb the urge to scream for joy. Although she counted Rachel, Beatrice, Abby and Carly as friends, it was Taryn who'd become her sister. The day she moved into the small apartment with Taryn it was as if they were sisters separated at birth. They liked the same movies and books—even their taste in music was very similar—and Taryn was as fastidious as she was. They'd hung out together on weekends whenever Taryn didn't have to babysit, and as elementary education majors they shared many of the same graduate courses. Taryn had accompanied her when the ABCs met for the farewell dinner for Beatrice, and she'd bonded quickly with the other women once they were aware that she was also a teacher.

Jessica stood on the lower step to the porch, staring at the dark and light shadows in the full moonlight. Taryn had left to return to New York the day before, and she missed talking with her friend and having her share cooking duties. Taryn was like a kid in a candy shop when she spent time in the greenhouses selecting vegetables and herbs for dishes that rivaled those in some DC soul food restaurants.

The familiar sound of a car's engine shattered the silence of the night. The outline of the Town Car came into view, and she held her breath at the same time Sawyer alighted from the rear of limo. He turned to look at her, and she swallowed a gasp when she saw his face. It was leaner, nearly gaunt, and lines of fatigue ringed his generous mouth. He set down his carry-on, lifted her off her feet and captured her mouth in a marauding kiss that sucked the air from her lungs.

He'd called her earlier that morning to tell her he was coming home later that night. Easing back and reaching up, she combed her fingers through his hair.

Touching and kissing Sawyer made her aware of how much she truly loved and missed him. Text messages, emails and sporadic telephone calls just were not enough for the flesh-and-blood man holding her to his heart. She pressed her mouth to his ear. "Come inside."

Sawyer loosened his hold on her waist, setting her on her feet. "Not yet. After being cooped up in an office for days I just want to sit outside for a while and breathe in some fresh air."

Jessica pulled her robe tighter around her body. "I'm going inside."

She knew intuitively he wanted to be alone. It was one thing to propose to her over the telephone and another to see her in person and pose the same question. Perhaps he'd asked her to marry him because he felt disconnected after they had just spent a glorious week together.

"I'll be in shortly." His voice floated after her as Jessica turned and went inside.

Sawyer needed time alone to reexamine the events going on his life. Coding Space Invaders: Total Domination had reenergized his interest in coming up with ideas for new video games. It was only when he lay in bed—alone—that his thoughts turned to Jessica. It took a lull from his work for him to consciously make time for her. And in a moment of weakness he'd asked her to marry him because he feared losing her. He loved her that much.

Pushing off the chair, he picked up the carry-on containing his laptop and walked into the house, closing and locking the door behind him. Bootsy left his bed, stretched and then came over to sniff him. Sawyer, leaning down, scratched him behind the ear. "How are you doing, little buddy?" The dog emitted a soft whine before ambling back to bed. It was apparent the puppy hadn't forgotten him.

Sawyer left his luggage on the floor next to the staircase and slowly mounted the stairs. He entered the hall bath, showered and, walking on bare feet, entered Jessica's bedroom. She lay with her back to him as he slipped into bed next to her.

Moving closer, he pressed a kiss to her silken shoulder. "I love you," he whispered. Sawyer marveled at how easy it was to tell Jessica he loved her.

"I love you, too."

"Are you up to talking about what I'd asked you?"

"What did you ask me?" she questioned.

He went completely still, not knowing if Jessica had forgotten his marriage proposal or if she was deliberately teasing him. "I asked you to marry me."

Jessica switched on the lamp on her side of the bed, and then turned over, her nose inches from his. "I love you, Sawyer. I love you more than any man I've ever met or known, but before I can accept your proposal I need to clear up a few things with you."

Resting an arm over her hip, he pulled her closer. "What do you want to know?"

"I met you for the first time two months ago, and that's hardly enough time for us to get to know each other well enough to consider marriage."

"Are you saying you'd like a long engagement?"

"Yes. I'd like us to wait at least until next May."

Sawyer replayed her suggestion in his head. Truthfully he did not want to wait ten months for Jessica to become his wife, but then he didn't want to lose her.

"Okay." He kissed the tip of her nose. "Tomorrow we'll go into town to look at rings."

Jessica looped her leg over his. "Thank you, Sawyer."

"Is something else bothering you?"

"Yes. Do you expect me to move to New York after we're married?"

"Of course," he said quickly. "New York is home base for my business."

"And Wickham Falls is where I teach. Doesn't that count in your equation?"

"Yes and no. You can always get a teaching position in New York. And you won't have to move until the end of the school."

"But what if I don't want to move or teach in New York?"

"Didn't you say you liked New York?" Sawyer asked.

"I like what it offers, but that doesn't mean I want to live there. I've moved so many times that I feel like a drifter. When I bought this house I made myself a promise that I would stay here until I died of old age. I don't have Beatrice's temperament, because when she married Jabari she knew his position with the bank required he go wherever he was transferred. They've moved three times in their ten-year marriage. Is that what's going to happen with us? Let me remind you that I'm not your mother, Sawyer, who allowed Henry to control every phase of her life until she had enough of his heavy-handedness."

"I'm not my father!"

"Did you hear yourself, Sawyer, when you said I can get a teaching position in New York? What if I told you to move your company to Wickham Falls?"

"That's not possible."

"Why not?" she asked.

"Because that would mean uprooting the lives of sixteen employees and my three partners."

"Am I not as important to you as your partners and employees?"

"You're more important."

"If that's the case, then you should try and understand why I want to live here—with you."

Sawyer pondered Jessica's entreaty because he was tired of spending every waking moment in the office while attempting to come up with new tech ideas. Coming home to The Falls and falling in love with Jessica had changed him, and for the better.

And it wasn't about making more money. He wanted what Thom and Elena had, and what Darius would have in the coming months when he married his longtime girlfriend. He wanted to share his life with a woman with whom he wanted to grow old. He also looked forward to starting a family. It was no longer about the here and now, but his future.

"Are you willing to compromise?"

"Compromise about what?" she asked.

"If you'll agree to a shorter engagement, then I promise we'll make The Falls our home. There may be times when I may have to go to New York, but…"

Jessica pressed her fingers to his lips, stopping his words. She removed her hand, her mouth replacing her fingers. "I agree."

Sawyer felt as if he'd won a small victory. If they married sooner rather than later, then he was content to go to New York on business and return to The Falls to live. "Give me a date as to when we'll marry, hopefully before the end of the year."

"What about the Thanksgiving weekend?"

His smile grew wider. "That sounds good to me. I guess that does it."

Jessica laughed softly. "Yes, it does." She buried her face in the hollow of his throat, unable to believe she just agreed to marry a man who was still a stranger. There were so many things she did not know about him, yet she knew if they lived together for the next fifty years they would never know everything about each other.

Without warning, Sawyer moved over her, one hand inching up her inner thigh. "What about babies?" he breathed in her ear.

Her pulse quickened as she felt his growing erection. "What about babies?"

"Do you want them?" he asked.

"Yes. But I'd like to start trying after our first an-niversary." Jessica felt the area between her legs grow moist as he cupped her breast, gently squeezing it until she arched off the mattress.

"I can't guarantee we'll begin with one, because twins show up in my family every other generation. My mother is a twin and you know about Dylan and Colin."

Her fingernails bit into his upper arms. "I'll divorce you if you saddle me with two badass twin boys."

Sawyer chuckled. "What if they're girls?"

"Of course our daughters will be princesses."

"Now, you know that's sexist." He rained a series of kisses down the column of her neck. "I want to make love to you so badly that I can't think straight."

"What's stopping you?" Jessica asked.

"I didn't bring protection with me."

"You don't need protection because I'm now on the pill. I didn't want to take the chance that we'd get a lit-tle crazy and have unprotected sex."

Wrapping her arms around his neck, she kissed Saw-yer; he increased the pressure of her mouth on his at the same time his breathing quickened. One hand pushed her nightgown up and over her hips while his other eased his erection into her body. Jessica did not have time to stifle a gasp when his hardness filled her.

His tongue slipped into her mouth, keeping perfect rhythm with his hips as he pushed into her over and over. Sawyer's hand was as busy as his mouth when he arched his lower body, his finger finding the tight nod-ule hidden in the downy hair at the apex of her thighs. The pad of his thumb massaged the engorged flesh, and she cried out shamelessly with the spasm of carnality shaking her from head to toe.

She felt herself sinking further and further into the morass of ecstasy, and then she stiffened with the explosive rush of orgasmic fulfillment sweeping through her. She screamed over and over until subsiding to long, surrendering moans of physical satiation, and as she closed her eyes she registered the rush of Sawyer's release bathing her throbbing flesh. Tears leaked from under her lids. The man she'd promised to marry possessed the power to assuage her physical need for him, but unknowingly he also had the power to hurt her.

They lay together, still joined, until their breathing resumed its normal rate. Jessica uttered a small protest when Sawyer withdrew from her. He turned off the lamp, then lay down to pull her hips against his groin. They lay like spoons and within minutes both had fallen asleep.

Jessica looped her arm through Sawyer's as they waited at baggage claim for his parents. The diamonds on her left hand were a constant reminder that in another four months she would exchange vows with a man she loved and trusted with her life.

She'd emailed her parents that she was engaged and planned a Thanksgiving wedding, and once they recovered from their Alaskan adventure she wanted them to come to Wickham Falls to meet her fiancé and his family. Sawyer did not tell Rachel of their engagement, because he wanted to tell his parents first.

Jessica sent Taryn a similar text with a ring emoji. "I see your mother," she said, pointing to her right.

Sawyer craned his neck. "Where's my father?"

Jessica glanced up at Sawyer, seeing lines of tension ringing his mouth. "He probably stopped to use the restroom," she said, hoping to allay his fear that something had happened to Henry.

Mara waved when she saw them next to the baggage carousel. She extended her arms, hugging Sawyer and kissing his cheek. Smoky-gray eyes in a sun-brown face shimmered with excitement. "I can't thank you enough for suggesting we celebrate our anniversary in Hawaii."

Sawyer glanced over her head. "Where's Dad?"

"He stopped to use the restroom."

Jessica met Mara's eyes. "Welcome home."

Mara reached for Jessica's hands, holding them firmly, and then her gaze lingered on the ring on Jessica's left hand. "You're engaged." The query was a statement.

Leaning forward, Jessica pressed her cheek to Mara's. "Yes. Sawyer and I plan to marry over the Thanksgiving weekend."

The tears filling Mara's eyes overflowed as she hugged Jessica so tightly she had difficulty breathing. "Oh…oh, sweet heaven. My prayers have been answered that he would find someone to soften his heart. I've always thought of you as family, and now we're really going to be family. And no more Mara. I insist you call me Mom."

Jessica struggled to free herself. "Thank you, Mom."

Taking a step back, Mara gave her son a long, lingering stare. "Don't hurt her or you'll have to deal with me."

Sawyer returned her stare. "I love Jessica too much to hurt her."

Henry joined them, his tanned face glowing with

good health. He hugged Sawyer, pounding his back and congratulating him on having the good sense to recognize an extraordinary woman when he met one. Jessica chatted with Mara about wanting a small intimate wedding with family and close friends, while Sawyer and Henry waited at the carousel to retrieve the luggage.

She'd decided she wanted Taryn as her maid of honor and Rachel as a bridal attendant. Sawyer talked about inviting the friends with whom he'd attended grad school and made tentative reservations for them to stay in the same hotel where they planned to hold the ceremony and reception.

The conversation was lively during the drive back to The Falls, Mara hinting that Rachel and Mason were seriously considering reconciliation and that their sons didn't want to come back to West Virginia because they loved living in Hawaii.

Sawyer maneuvered up the driveway to Jessica's house, meeting her eyes. "I'm going to drop you off first, then take my folks home. I'll see you later tonight."

Jessica waited for Sawyer to come around and assist her out the Jeep. When he mentioned seeing her later she wondered if he planned to spend the night now that his parents were home. "Why don't you hang out with your parents tonight?" she suggested. "It's their first night back and I'm certain you'll have a lot to talk about."

Sawyer frowned. "Are you getting tired of me coming over?"

"Of course not," she said quickly. Jessica rested a hand on his jaw. "I love you, Sawyer, and there's never a time when I don't want us to be together. I'm just thinking of your folks, who've probably missed you.

After all, it hasn't been that long since you've come back home."

Sawyer placed his larger hand over hers. "What did I do to deserve someone like you?"

Lowering his head, he kissed her. Jessica gave him a gentle shove. "Now go, because Harry and Mara are probably exhausted from their flight."

She didn't tell Sawyer she felt uncomfortable with their public display of affection—especially in the presence of her future in-laws. She waved to Sawyer's parents, then unlocked the door and walked into the house.

Her parents had returned from their trip a week ago, but she hadn't heard from them as to when they planned to come to West Virginia. Reaching for the wall phone, she dialed their number. "Hello, Mama," she said upon hearing her mother's dulcet voice. "I decided to call because I want to know when you and Daddy are coming."

"We're coming, but first your father has to get over a cold. He's been hacking so bad that I finally insisted he see a doctor. He claims it's the damp weather here and I agree with him. We're thinking about moving back East."

Jessica went completely still, the rapid beating of her heart echoing in her ears. She had always hoped her parents would consider moving east of the Mississippi. "Are you serious?"

"Quite serious," Christina confirmed. "Although Seattle is beautiful, we've never really connected with the city's climate or lifestyle."

"Where are you thinking of moving?"

"Virginia. I'm partial to Georgetown and your father prefers Alexandria."

Jessica clapped a hand over her mouth to stifle

shrieks of joy. Having her parents within driving distance was an answer to all her silent prayers. "Both are wonderful neighborhoods, and I'm going to sound very selfish when I say I'm going to love having you live closer to me."

"It's the same with me and your daddy. There are quite a few condos and townhouses for seniors, so that's what we're having the real estate agent look for."

"How long do you think it's going to take for you to sell your place?" Jessica asked.

"Not long, because there's a wait list to get into this community. Folks like that it's a gated area."

"Do you think you'll move before my wedding?"

"That's what we're hoping."

Jessica did not want to believe everything in her life was falling into place. She was engaged to a man she looked forward to sharing her future with. Her parents had decided to move to Virginia, and that meant no more cross-country trips. She hung up as joy wrapped around her, filling her with a gentle peace from which she did not want to escape.

Sawyer sat at the kitchen table with his mother. "You're questioning my decision to marry Jessica?"

Mara shook her head. "Not your decision to marry her, but wanting to make her your wife after only knowing her for a few months."

He closed his eyes for a few seconds. "I knew there was something special about Jessica the minute I laid eyes on her. At first I thought it was her beauty, but when I forced myself to look beyond the obvious I realized she has what I'd been searching for in all of the women

I'd ever dated. And don't look at me like that, Mom," he said when a frown appeared between her eyes.

"Like what?" Mara asked, her frown disappearing.

"As if I don't know what I'm about to get in to."

"Do you, Sawyer? Marriage is a commitment that's not to be taken lightly. Some folks believe if it doesn't work out, then they'll just get a divorce. It's not for a couple of months or years, but a lifetime. There were times when I thought of leaving your father because he wasn't the easiest man to live with, but when I thought about my children growing up without a father I knew I had to stay. And what saved our marriage was Henry going away for months at a time. I figured I could put up with him for the few weeks he was at home, so I just bit my tongue and endured his chronic complaining because I resigned myself that I'd never be able to change him."

"But he did change," Sawyer stated.

"That's because, in the end, he blamed himself for sending you away."

"He didn't send me away. I left of my own accord. But now I'm back to stay."

Mara's eyes widened, seemingly shocked by this disclosure. "You're going to live here after you're married?"

"Yes. Even though Jessica doesn't want to move to New York, she's okay with me leaving her if I have to go there on business."

"What about your place in New York?"

"I intend to hold on to it. It wouldn't pay for me to give it up because Jessica and I can use it as our hotel whenever we decide to visit or vacation there. And if you and Dad ever go up to New York, you'll have some-place to stay."

"Do you realize your life will mirror your father's? You'll have to leave your family to earn a living."

Sawyer paused, pondering his mother's statement. She was only half right. "My partners and I are think-ing of going public, and if we do then I'll sell my share in the company and look for a position in or around Charleston."

"Can't you find one closer to The Falls?"

"I won't know that until I go online to search for companies looking for a software engineer. But that's something I don't have to concern myself with now." He stood up. "I'm sorry to run, but I need to make some phone calls." Mara rose with him. "And I'm going to take a shower, then crawl into bed."

Rounding the table, Sawyer pressed a kiss to his mother's forehead. "I'll see you later."

Chapter Fourteen

July gave way to August, and Jessica realized there were only four days before the first day of school for students, and two of those days were set aside for continuing education for faculty.

Sitting in a rocker on the porch at his parents' house, Jessica gave Sawyer a sidelong glance. Eyes closed, he reclined on the porch swing.

"I probably won't see you for the next three days because I have continuing education for two days, and then I'll have to prep for the school opening the following day."

Sawyer opened his eyes. "I suppose once school starts we won't see much of each other during the week until we're married."

"There's always the weekends," Jessica reminded him.

"I know you keep to your hard-and-fast schedule during the school year, but would you consider taking the weekends off to take short road trips with me?"

Jessica sat straight. "Where would we go?"

Sawyer lifted a broad shoulder. "Maybe we can take in DC, or if it's a long weekend we can fly down to San Juan or St. Thomas for a change of scene."

She sprang to her feet, raced over to him and threw her arms around his neck. "Yes," she whispered. "The Friday before Labor Day is an OS Day, so there's no school. That will give us four full days to go buck wild."

"What's OS?" Sawyer asked.

"Outside School Environment. I'll show you my school calendar for the year when you come back to the house." Jessica had begun to refer to the house on Porterfield Lane as *the house* or *our home* because once she and Sawyer were married they would share not only their lives but also their possessions. Sitting beside Sawyer, Jessica laced her fingers through his. "Are we going to take a honeymoon?"

"Yes. But that can't happen until your school is on holiday. The Christmas break is preferable to Easter because one of my friends is getting married that week."

"Where do you want to honeymoon?" she asked.

"Anyplace that's warm in December."

"I'd like to go to Punta Cana."

His eyebrows lifted questioningly. "Have you ever been there?"

"Yes. I went there on spring break during my first year at college, and I've always wanted to go back."

"Punta Cana it is." Personally, he would've preferred going to the South Pacific, but that was someplace they could visit during the summer break.

They sat together, each lost in their thoughts as the

sun sank lower on the horizon. Jessica stirred first. "I have to go and let Bootsy out."

Sawyer rose to his feet, easing her up with him. He dropped a kiss on her curls. He'd cut his hair earlier that summer, while Jessica had decided to let hers grow out. He walked her to her vehicle. Pulling her into an embrace, he stared over her head at the massive oak tree he'd climbed countless times as a boy. "I'll see you Friday night."

He held open the door as she climbed up into the SUV, and despite the warmth of the early evening he felt a cold shiver sweep over his exposed skin. Sawyer was more than aware their relationship would change now that school was scheduled to start up again, and that he and Jessica wouldn't have the luxury of being together whenever they chose.

Jessica pulled into her designated parking space in the faculty lot. She recognized many of the returning teachers as they waved and called out to one another. This year would be different because Beatrice wouldn't be there, and she would be teaching fifth grade instead of second.

The orientation was held in the high school's auditorium before teachers went to their respective buildings to set up their classrooms for the first day. She found a seat next to Logan, both exchanging wide smiles when she noticed the gold wedding band on his hand while he pointed to the diamond on her left. "Congratulations," she whispered.

He leaned closer, their shoulders touching. "Thanks. Is he someone I know?"

"Probably not," she whispered. "But you'll get to meet him whenever we have a social function."

"He lives in The Falls?"

"Yes. In fact, he was born here."

Conversations ended abruptly when the district's superintendent stood at the podium, gently tapping the mic. Seated on the stage were the principals of the elementary, middle and high schools. There were also empty chairs set aside for the new hires. Jessica waved to Carly and Abby when they sat down in the row in front of hers.

The superintendent began with the same speech Jessica had heard over the years; she wondered if the woman had memorized it. Smiling, she handed the microphone to the high school principal, Adrien Silver, who welcomed all of the returning teachers before introducing the new hires assigned to his school.

Dr. Silver extended his hand to those assembled. "I'd like all of the members of the grant committee to stand up." Jessica and Logan rose with the others. "Due to your ceaseless commitment in securing a grant for our technology lab, I'd like everyone to know not only were we awarded the grant, but we received twice as much as we initially requested." He held up a hand to halt the thunderous applause. "The result is we're now able to create a technology department. None of us wanted to lose the expertise of the consultant instrumental in securing the grant, so we decided to invite him to join our faculty. Not only will he become the department head, but he also happens to be an alumnus of our high school. Ladies and gentlemen, I'd like Sawyer Middleton to take the stage."

Jessica closed her eyes, unable to believe what she

was seeing as Sawyer strolled onto the stage, looking elegant in a tailored navy-blue suit. He shook hands with Dr. Silver, and then sat on the chair nearest the podium as deafening applause filled the auditorium.

It unnerved her to see her fiancé sitting on the stage. Not once had he hinted that he'd interviewed for a position at the high school. Unconsciously, she twisted the diamond ring around and around her finger. She'd fallen in love with him, shared her body with him and promised to share her future with him because she trusted him.

Carly turned, giving her an incredulous stare. "Did you know your fiancé was going to be a department head?"

Jessica wanted to tell her friend that she knew but decided to tell the truth. "No."

Abby snorted delicately. "Talk about surprises. I'd like to be a fly on the wall when he gets home."

No, you wouldn't, Jessica thought. She'd sent her colleagues texts that she was engaged to Sawyer and wanted them to save the date for their post-Thanksgiving nuptials, but unless Sawyer had a good reason for blindsiding her she was seriously contemplating not going through with it.

Somehow Jessica managed to make it through the entire orientation without losing her composure. She followed the middle school teachers as they walked the connecting hallway to their building. She had no intention of starting their lives together with them keeping secrets from each other and used all of her pent-up frustration to rearrange textbooks and pamphlets.

The time of reckoning came when Jessica returned home to find Sawyer in a pair of jeans sitting on the top step of the porch. He rose slowly as she walked up the steps.

Dipping his head, he kissed her cheek. "I thought you would've been home before now."

Jessica didn't bother to meet his eyes as she opened the door. "I wanted to rearrange my classroom." She scratched Bootsy behind his ears when he came over to greet her. She dropped her tote on the footstool in the living room and sat on the sofa. "Sawyer, we have to talk."

Sawyer sat on the love seat and leaned down to pick up Bootsy. "I know what you want to talk about."

"I didn't know you could read minds," Jessica drawled sarcastically.

A hint of a smile parted his lips. "I can't, but I think I know you well enough to know what you want to talk about. You're a little ticked off because I didn't tell you that I'll be teaching at your school."

Jessica slowly shook her head. "It's not my school, Sawyer. If it was, then I would've known before I had to find out with everyone else that you'll head the technology department. Did it amuse you to keep me in the dark, or were you sworn to secrecy?"

Sawyer crossed his arms over his chest. "I wasn't sworn to secrecy."

"Then why didn't you tell me?"

"I wanted to surprise you."

"In other words, you were hiding the fact that you'll be teaching here as payback because I asked you if you expect me to move to New York after we're married. I remember your response. *Of course, because New York is home base for my business.*"

He frowned. "There's no payback."

"You did more than surprise me. I was embarrassed because Carly asked me if I knew you were going to become a department head and I didn't lie when I said no. What hurts is that you didn't trust me enough to let me know what's going on in your life. What else are you hiding from me?" He stared at her, unblinking. "I wanted a longer engagement so I would get to know you better, and now I'm pissed because I should've followed my own instincts." She paused, gathering her thoughts. "Right now I'm so confused."

Lowering his arms, Sawyer leaned forward. "Why?"

"Because you're a fraud, and I will not pledge my future to a man who can't tell me what's going on in his life."

Sawyer was so still he could've been carved out of stone. "I've told you everything, Jessica. You know who I am, what I'm worth and that I've made certain if anything happens to me you'll have enough money to live on for the rest of your life."

"It's not about money," she countered. "It's about trust, and without it we have nothing." She ran a hand over her face. "Please go. Right now I need to be alone. And forget about us going away together over the Labor Day weekend."

Sawyer was numbed by the realization he'd possibly lost the only woman he loved because he'd wanted to surprise her. Sawyer forced himself to stand and walk out of the house where he'd planned to live with his wife.

Sawyer drove back to his parents' house, exceeding the speed limit and swerving to avoid hitting a dog ambling across the road. He stalked into the house, slamming the door violently.

"Please don't tell me they fired you before the first day of school," Mara teased when he stalked into the kitchen.

"That's not funny!" he shouted.

"Don't you dare raise your voice to me, Sawyer Travers Middleton! I had enough of that from your father, and I refuse to take it from my children."

Sawyer felt properly chastised. "I'm sorry, Mom. I'm upset about something."

"Is that something named Jessica?"

He froze, wondering if Jessica had called Mara. "How did you know?"

"Because I'm a mother who happens to know her children better than they believe I do. I knew Rachel was going to reconcile with Mason once she agreed to go to Hawaii, and I also knew you were smitten with Jessica the instant I saw you together. Sit down, son, and talk to me."

Sawyer pulled out a chair for his mother and sat next to her. He told her about not telling Jessica that he had joined the school district as the head of the newly formed technology department.

"I know you wanted to surprise her, Sawyer, but instead of surprising Jessica, you blindsided her."

He nodded. "I know that now."

"You need to apologize to her and promise never to do something like this again."

"There's nothing to apologize for."

Mara shook her head. "You and your father are one of a kind—stubborn as mules. And if you don't do what you have to do to get your personal life in order, then you're going to end up old, lonely and angry. You can't do whatever you want and the hell with everyone else. There are two people in your relationship—you and Jessica. And if you don't consider her feelings whenever you decide something, then you're going to lose her. Give her time to cool off and then go and apologize. It will not make you less of a man if you say you're sorry."

Sawyer knew Mara was right, even though he still believed he had nothing to apologize for. His footfalls were slow and heavy as he climbed the staircase to his attic bedroom. He fell across the bed, staring up at the ceiling. How, he mused, had it been so easy for him to become so successful in his career, yet his personal life had lagged so far?

He thought it ironic that he had to come home to find a woman who made him want to forsake the big city and all it offered to settle down in a town with forty-eight hundred residents and two traffic lights. He would give Jessica a week to cool off before approaching her again. Hopefully she would be in a better mood to hear him out.

Five days later, Sawyer and the newly hired IT technician installed Wi-Fi and set up servers, and then opened cartons of computers. They placed them on the computer tables in the recently painted technology lab. He hadn't run into Jessica because he'd spent all his time in the high school. It would be a while before he and his assistant would set up computers and smart-boards in the middle and elementary school buildings. The school board had revised the budget to update re-wiring the entire campus to accommodate the new electronic equipment.

He missed seeing Jessica, his need never more acute than when he lay in bed—alone. Mara didn't broach the subject of Jessica, and for that he was eternally grateful. He was noncommittal with Rachel when she emailed him asking if he was involved in the wedding plans, and he told her she would have to talk to Jessica about it. After all, it was Jessica who'd put their engagement on hold.

Jessica had just finished folding the clothes she'd taken from the dryer when she heard Bootsy's frantic barking; someone was at the door. Rushing down the staircase she peered through the security eye to find Taryn's grinning face staring back at her.

She opened the door, and within seconds she and Taryn were hugging as if they hadn't seen each other in years. Peering around her friend's shoulder, she noticed the gleaming black late-model Nissan Pathfinder parked behind her vehicle.

"You bought a new car?"

Taryn's ponytail swayed as her head moved up and down like a bobblehead doll. "I had to, because my hoopty would never have survived the drive. I would've lost the transmission somewhere between here and Baltimore."

Smiling, Jessica opened the door wider. "Come in." She had invited Taryn to come visit her for the Labor Day weekend because she really needed to see her friend. Taryn brushed past her, flopped down on the love seat and kicked off her espadrilles. "I decided to come a couple of days early so I can spend some time with you, because I don't know when we'll get the chance to get together once my school year begins. I brought some bridal magazines so you can select which style of gown you want."

Jessica sat down next to Taryn and held her hand. "I don't think I'm getting married."

"What?" The single word exploded from Taryn's mouth. She listened in total shock as Jessica recounted what had happened between her and Sawyer, including his teaching at her school and donating the money for the technology department.

"How would you feel marrying a man who can't open up to you?" she asked Taryn.

"Maybe he's like my brother."

Lines of confusion creased Jessica's forehead. "What are you talking about? Your brother is a salesman for a pharmaceutical company."

"That's what we tell everyone, but in reality my brother is a navy SEAL. My sister-in-law freaks out every time he tells her he has to go work. Sometimes he's away for a couple of weeks or longer, and she's a basket case until he walks back through the door."

Jessica blew out a breath. "Well, I know Sawyer isn't a SEAL because he was in the army."

"What if he's an Army Ranger or Delta Force?"

"He's not active military, Taryn."

Taryn chewed her lip. "Do you still love him?"

Taryn's question caught Jessica completely off guard. "Of course I still love him."

"Then call and let him know."

Jessica exhaled a slow, audible sigh. "He knows I love him."

"Did you give him back the ring?"

"No."

"Then put that puppy on, call your man and tell him

you want to marry him. I know you believe he deceived you, but you have to know he loves you and he's willing to do anything to make you happy. How many men do you know would do that for a woman?"

"I don't know, but what I want is for him to apologize."

"And if he doesn't?" Taryn asked.

"Then I'm not going to marry him. Sawyer can't do whatever he wants because he deems it. He doesn't realize he isn't the only one in this relationship. I'd never make decisions that will impact our lives or future without discussing it with him."

Taryn shook her head. "It looks as if he blew it big time."

"Go get your bags and after you're settled we'll talk."

Sawyer sat in the family room with his parents. He had called Jessica at six that morning, waking her up, and asking to meet so they could talk. He'd hardly recognized her voice when she told him he could come over later that evening. It had taken him nearly a week to think about his mother's accusation that he was just like his father. And after some serious introspection he realized she wasn't that far off. He had asked Jessica to marry him, and then put a ring on her finger, before she was given an opportunity to think about it. Then he had suggested she move to New York because that's where he did business, but then offered to move to Wickham Falls almost immediately when she resisted. It was only when she'd accused him of being like Henry that he knew he had to compromise or lose her completely. But he had lost her when he decided not to tell her that he would not only become her husband but her colleague.

Rising to his feet, he kissed his mother and then patted his father's shoulder. "I have to go and meet Jessica."

"Give her my love," Mara called out.

"Will do."

He pulled into the driveway of Jessica's home and found her sitting on the porch with another woman. Jessica came to her feet, walking down to meet him, a mysterious smile softening her lips. His gaze shifted to her left hand. She was wearing the ring. He pulled her close, burying his face in her fragrant curls.

"I'm sorry, babe. I promise as long as I live I'll never hide anything from you."

"But…"

His mouth covered hers, stopping whatever she intended to say.

"I've missed you so much, babe."

"And I've missed you, too."

They sprang apart at the distinctive sound of someone clearing their throat. Jessica eased back at Taryn's approach. "Sawyer, I'd like you to meet my Howard roommate, Taryn Robinson."

He smiled at the tall, attractive woman, extending his hand. "It's a pleasure to meet you." He was slightly taken aback when she ignored his hand and kissed his cheek.

"You don't have to be so formal," Taryn teased. "I'm going inside and leave you two to talk. Later," she crooned.

Waiting until Taryn went inside the house, Sawyer curved his arms around Jessica's waist. His eyes moved slowly and lovingly over her face. "I can't believe what I've done to you when I know how much trust means to you. And you're right when you accuse me of being like my father, but I'm begging you to let me know when I start acting like him."

She placed her fingers over his mouth. "You don't have to beg. Just think before you act. We're not going to always agree on everything, but we can compromise. You did when I told you I didn't want to move to New York, and I did when I agreed to a shorter engagement."

He nodded. "You're right. I'm sorry I didn't tell you I was hired to head the technology department, and I'm sorry you were embarrassed when your friends asked if you knew."

Jessica smiled. "I accept your apology if you promise not to do again."

He picked her up and swung her around. "I promise."

She tightened her hold on his neck. "I love you, Sawyer, and I want more than anything else in this world to become your wife."

"You don't want it any more than I want to become your husband. I want to marry you, raise our children in this house and grow old with you."

She kissed the bridge of his nose. "That goes double for me."

A smile lit up Sawyer's eyes. "I would like to renovate the basement for entertaining with a downstairs kitchen, as well as put in a backyard waterfall, filling it with koi. But only with your approval."

"Of course I approve."

He brushed a kiss over her parted lips. "Let's go inside. We need to discuss what we have to do to make our wedding a rousing success."

Four months later, Jessica knew her father could feel her trembling as he covered her hand draped over the sleeve of his suit jacket. It was her wedding day, and friends and family members had gathered in the room where she would exchange vows with a man she hadn't believed she could love as much as she did. Rachel, her sons and their father had flown in looking tanned and happy to be back in The Falls. Beatrice and Jabari had surprised her when they arrived from Denver earlier that morning, and her parents, who'd moved into their Georgetown condo in late October, had spent the past two weeks with her, her mother working closely with the wedding planner to put the finishing touches on the small, elegant affair.

Jessica curbed the urge to touch the strand of magnificent golden sea pearls draped around her neck and in her ears. After the rehearsal dinner Sawyer had led her to his hotel suite and given her his wedding gift. She was just as shocked with her gift as he was with his. She'd presented him with a pair of monogrammed gold cufflinks. He'd laughed hysterically, declaring he would treasure them forever.

Russell Calhoun gently squeezed her fingers. "Are you ready, princess?"

It wasn't the first time that he'd asked her if she was ready to marry Sawyer after a whirlwind courtship. "Yes, Daddy."

She hadn't realized as a young girl when she played with other girls her age in her neighborhood, and they'd pretend they were married to rich, handsome men, lived in wonderful homes, and their dolls were their children, that in time their playacting would become a reality for her.

A member of the hotel staff opened the door as the "Wedding March" filled the room and Jessica processed in on her father's arm, her gaze fixed on Sawyer. He'd selected his father as his best man, and Thom and Darius as his attendants. Her gaze shifted to Taryn and Rachel, both resplendent in gold and orange silk-satin peau de soie. The colors of yellow, orange and chocolate brown were in keeping with a seasonal autumn theme. Sawyer's boutonniere of orange blossoms matched the tiny yellow rosebuds threaded through her loose curls. She caught a brief glimpse of her mother in a flattering black-and-orange silk coatdress. Christina blotted the corners of her eyes with a tissue.

The officiant met her eyes, giving her an imperceptible nod. "Who gives this woman in marriage?"

Russell stood straighter. "I do." His deep voice reverberated throughout the room. That said, he placed Jessica's hand on Sawyer's outstretched palm and moved over to stand beside his wife.

Jessica couldn't stop the heat suffusing her face when Sawyer whispered, "I never believed I'd be this blessed."

She managed to turn her attention to the pastor of the church where she and Sawyer attended services. What occurred next became a blur as she repeated her vows, slipped the wedding band on Sawyer's finger and then returned to reality when she felt his mouth on hers to seal their nuptials.

When she turned to face those who'd come to witness her wedding to Wickham Falls' native son, she knew it was a place both would call home for the rest of their lives.

* * * * *

MILLS & BOON®

Cherish™

EXPERIENCE THE ULTIMATE RUSH OF FALLING IN LOVE

A sneak peek at next month's titles...

In stores from 13th July 2017:

- **The Boss's Fake Fiancée** – Susan Meier *and*
  Mummy and the Maverick (Mommy and the Maverick) – Meg Maxwell
- **The Runaway Bride and the Billionaire** – Kate Hardy *and* **Vegas Wedding, Weaver Bride** – Allison Leigh

In stores from 27th July 2017:

- **The Millionaire's Redemption** – Therese Beharrie *and* **Do You Take This Cowboy?** – Vicki Lewis Thompson
- **Captivated by the Enigmatic Tycoon** – Bella Bucannon *and* **AWOL Bride** – Victoria Pade

Just can't wait?
Buy our books online before they hit the shops!
www.millsandboon.co.uk

Also available as eBooks.

MILLS & BOON®

Why shop at millsandboon.co.uk?

Each year, thousands of romance readers
find their perfect read at millsandboon.co.uk.
That's because we're passionate about
bringing you the very best romantic fiction.
Here are some of the advantages of
shopping at www.millsandboon.co.uk:

* **Get new books first**—you'll be able to buy
  your favourite books one month before they
  hit the shops

* **Get exclusive discounts**—you'll also be
  able to buy our specially created monthly
  collections, with up to 50% off the RRP

* **Find your favourite authors**—latest news,
  interviews and new releases for all your
  favourite authors and series on our website,
  plus ideas for what to try next

* **Join in**—once you've bought your favourite
  books, don't forget to register with us to rate,
  review and join in the discussions

Visit **www.millsandboon.co.uk**
for all this and more today!